W9-AEB-110

The Notebook *of Lost* Things

The Notebook
of *Lost* Things

M E G A N   S T A F F E L

SOHO

Published by

Soho Press Inc.
853 Broadway
New York, NY 10003

Library of Congress Cataloging-in-Publication Data

Staffel, Megan
    The notebook of lost things : a novel / Megan Staffel.
      p. cm.
    ISBN 1-56947-160-6 (alk. paper)
    I. Title
    PS3569, T16N67   1999   98-43484
    813'.54--dc21   CIP

10 9 8 7 6 5 4 3 2 1

For my parents

I am indebted to a book called *Ordeal by Fire*, a firsthand account by a survivor of the Dresden bombing, Anne Wahle, as told to Ralph Tunley. I am also indebted to Elizabeth and Catherine Gulacsy, who told me about their experiences in Germany during the war and read portions of the manuscript. I want to thank Sandra Singer, who helped with German, and Matthew Goodman, Mary Elsie Robertson, and the Sunday group, who read drafts of the manuscript. My deep appreciation to Elizabeth Sheinkman, my agent, and Fred Busch.

One

~~~

At the farm on Eastern Road where Helene lived with William Swick, October was the month for killing chickens. Chicken death was the right activity for an October afternoon when the last of the insects buzzed in the high grass and the air was filled with leaf dust and drifting seeds. The afternoon sun slanted down over the hillside and even though it was warm, it was a distant, equivocal warmth because in the rot and sludge at the surface of the earth there was a trickle of something cold that overnight would get even more sluggish as it slipped into the medial stage between liquid and ice.

In the human world, things were more definite. There was the same slow ceaseless movement from one condition to the next but against the abruptness of certain human events, it was easy to overlook. Two years ago in October, Helene's mother had died. One year ago in October, her brother, Gunter, had packed his belongings and driven to San Francisco. That left only her and William Swick—her "Uncle" William—to occupy the big drafty house and somehow fill the portion of land on Eastern Road between the two bridges, a distance of a half mile that used to be hay field and pasture and now was uncut grasses.

After her mother died, Gunter had been the one to kill the chickens. Now the job came to her. Gunter did ten chickens on four days, preferring to get it over with quickly. She did one a day for as many days as it took. That way it became ordinary. She could think as she handled the bloody carcass, sift through the problems. There were always problems. The first and most pressing was her boyfriend, Harry, who in the month of October had turned fifty-seven, eighteen years older than she was. She thought he was contemptible. Were he to have a heart attack suddenly, she would be relieved. And yet...

She caught a hen behind the chicken shed and as she held it in her arms she watched the black chicken eye taking in the hills and trees around them. Under her fingers, she could feel the pumping of its heart. She told the hen that one day she, Helene, would also die and she knew she would be just as scared as the hen was. She carried it to the patio and laid her head across the guillotine and locked her neck into place with the metal bar so it couldn't wiggle out. It would be the same for her one day, she told the chicken. She also wouldn't want to leave the earth that had surrounded her for so many years with this thickness of sounds and smells and textures. Just like the chicken's eyes, her eyes would roam the brown fields because it hadn't been enough, and what little there had been was so full and real and overpowering that it seemed inconceivable that it would end. How could it possibly?

Death was all around her, and yet Helene needed to rehearse it once to herself before she could kill the chicken. So she thought of how frost had killed the squash and tomato plants in the garden whose tall, luxuriant foliage in August had draped over the other vegetables. The goldenrod in the field, at first a brilliant yellow, was now gray and brown. The leaves on the skunk cabbage, thick and green in the spring, had shriveled up and turned the color of smoke. All around her there were endings, diminishments. And yet, a creature wanted to go on.

The chicken cackled. Without hesitation, she brought the blade down. The head tumbled off and the body tumbled over into her hands. Then it picked itself up and ran about, still cackling, the blood spurting out of the ragged hole where the head used to be, the wings flapping up and down uselessly. It was only nature, only the muscles' inability to stop doing what they had been doing every second of every day since the beak had made the first crack in the shell and the grand movements began. Helene ran after it, scooped it up, and held it against her apron until it was still. Then, holding the feet, she dunked it in the kettle of hot water to loosen the feathers. She pulled it out, dripping water, smelling of blood, and tied it to the maple tree, which looked like a molting chicken itself with half its leaves on the ground and the other half still hanging off its branches.

In the early days, she would hold the chicken in front of a log on the ground, Gunter would keep its neck down between two nails with a stick, Uncle William would swing the ax, and her mother, appearing at the end with the kettle of hot water, would pluck and clean the carcass. Now, with Gunter in San Francisco, her mother someplace behind the curtains of the visible world, which the chicken was just now stepping through (no doubt pecking as it always did), and Uncle William down at the bookstore, dressing a chicken was a one-woman operation.

She made the first slit with the point of her knife. The skin squeaked as the metal sliced through the layer of flesh and outside air rushed into the sealed space of the chicken's cavity. She lifted the skin up, a flap with a thick yellow lining of fat, and put her hand into the warm insides. So hot. It was just what Harry said when he first entered her. "You're so hot." Yes, she'd tell him dreamily, yes. Carefully, she felt around the intestines and gently lifted them up into the sunlight. Against the yellow October afternoon the blue-gray guts spilling down onto the mass of feathers seemed out of place. The liver was lovely, though; she set it and the heart aside for Uncle, who was ignoble enough to crave another creature's organs. She supposed he would want the gizzard too, which she broke off from the intestines and set aside. Not even Uncle William would eat the lungs, curiously flat and insubstantial organs that she had to scrape out of the chest cavity. The other chickens moved around to the barn side and, seeing her on the patio, came running over. One of them would find the head and carry it around proudly to show it off, then in private peck at the closed eyes and the lumps of dried blood. The others would eat all the scraps that had fallen under the tree, everything except the feathers, which the wind, just now rolling down the valley, would lift up and scatter.

• • •

In the kitchen, Helene rinsed out the bird. She got the butcher knife from the drawer and cut off the feet. These she scrubbed with the vegetable brush, keeping them under water to flush out the dirt. They were bright yellow and leathery. She handled them with respect because even though the chicken's soul was no longer present, she believed that was where it had resided. She laid the feet between the legs and slipped the bird into a large plastic bag.

Her soul was in her cheeks, which turned red in cold weather, or at sex, or with booze. Her deepest feelings rode in her cheeks, which grew splotchy, giving her away when she was going to cry. Harry's soul was in his back, where he couldn't see it.

Outside, the chickens were still pecking in the puddle of guts. She emptied the kettle and turned it upside-down next to the house. The rope remained on the tree year after year and the guillotine stayed out until the end of the month, when Uncle William would scrub the rust off the blade, oil the hinge, and wrap his invention in a flannel sheet for the next season. The wind stirred up the feathers lying on the ground and ruffled the grass. The leaves lay under the maple like a huge yellow skirt, but they were too heavy with dew for the breeze to move. They mirrored the sun, which spotted the cement patio and made the peeling clapboard on the house look beautiful. The gutter that had fallen off last winter was still on the ground and the section that would probably fall off in the first autumn storm dangled from its one hanger. But the disrepair of the property was only a part of the general swelling up of nature on a parcel of land where cows hadn't grazed for many years and neither a tractor nor a chainsaw interrupted the constant drone of insects. The hills lifted up on either side of the house. Their wooded slopes had always been too steep for the tractor and in the days when Uncle William was a boy and his father managed the farm, there were always a couple of workhorses to skid the logs out of the forest. But the horses were gone now, the barn had settled into the land, and one day it would lean too recklessly into the arms of the wind and then it would collapse, scattering a century's accumulation of hay dust.

Helene watched the sun riding up the sky in the East towards noon. Past the curtain behind recognizable things, past the sun and the barn and the hillside, were the chickens she had killed so far and her mother and all the other dead she didn't know about. In the West was San Francisco where cars and trucks rumbled across Gunter's path. She and William were the only ones left here in the center.

Two

⚬⚬

Paris, New York, was the halfway point between Sharon and Goose Pond. It was a spot of convergence, a place where the past overlapped the present, where desire met futility, where ideas that were grand and beautiful ran into the hard facts of economics and got flattened. The land and weather took dominance and the result was that only those with imagination survived.

It hadn't always been like that. In other decades, the projects that men and women devised to make money or to entertain themselves were not so often ill-fated or paltry. In 1885, Paris was the center for a hundred and twenty-five dairy farms that were spread out over the countryside. The village was prosperous and bustling. In 1912, it was the location of Ontario Cheese and Swick Ceramics, companies that employed hundreds of people and affected the economy county-wide. There was an opera house, a women's hat store, a hotel. The homes on Main Street looked good; they were three-story dwellings with gingerbread around the porches and carriage houses sitting at the end of wide green lawns. The most ostentatious belonged to Elias Fenton, the attorney. It was painted a yellow that rivaled the sun on a warm day in the summer and had a mansard roof, something unheard-of in that part of the country. It was made with slate brought in from Pennsylvania on the train instead of the cheaper local terra-cotta tile. The slate was pink and gray, far more subdued and elegant than the thick orange tile on the neighboring houses.

At one end of Main Street the road circled the park, setting it off from the business district and showcasing the seven majestic elm trees that had been planted in 1826. The horse and wagon traffic in the circle, as it was called, was constant on a Saturday afternoon when families from the farms outside of Paris came into town to do their shopping and make an appearance at the hardware store or the beautician's or the restaurant, and the people from the village chose to drive their carriages downtown rather than walk. Still, despite all of that traffic, children darted from one side of the street to the other fearlessly, and summer days were filled with the sounds of horses nickering, wagon wheels rolling too quickly over the old dirt roads, and the constant buzzing of flies that grew fat and numerous on the rich diet of droppings.

By 1937, the traffic had changed to automobiles. A pagoda was erected in the park for Saturday evening band concerts. No one attended opera anymore and, in 1941, the opera house was turned into a library. The elm trees grew sickly in the fifties and were cut down by '59, and a decade later, the fuller, more circular shapes of sugar maples provided shade for the picnic tables.

In 1967, Baldwin Mercantile, the department store that had occupied the building in the block between Elm and Owen since 1922, closed. A clothing store moved in a year later. It was called Ann's Casual Wear but it soon went out of business because it couldn't compete with the larger shops in Sharon. The building was empty for five years and then in 1970, Smokes and Jokes, a store that sold newspapers, magazines, comic books, tobacco, and fishing and hunting supplies, opened on the bottom floor. The upper floor of the building stayed empty.

A bar called Better Days occupied the storefront across from Smokes and Jokes. It had been there since 1940. Paris Hardware, which had a cabinet on its back wall that consisted of one hundred and thirty-nine wooden drawers, each one filled with the nail or screw pictured on the card at the front, opened its doors in 1923 and did a small but brisk business through the first part of the century when it had a sideline of farm supplies. In 1950 it expanded into the building next to it, dropped the agrarian goods, and stocked kitchenware instead, including all the items required for home canning and freezing. Sullivan Paris, Jr., the son of the store's original owner, worked at the cash register from 1944 to 1975 and he watched the Fenton homestead across the street change in appearance over the years as it went from the town's grandest residence to a boarding house, then to apartments owned by a Paris native who covered it with aluminum siding, retired to Florida, and was unwilling thereafter to spend money on repairs. With the gutters fallen off and the original roof green with moss, it turned into a glorious spectacle one night as

Sullivan was locking the hardware store. There was something red reflected in the glass on the door from which he was just removing the key. So he turned around and saw the French doors on the house across the street whoosh open and fire leap out onto the porch and in one terrific wave of flame melt the rotten columns and the broken steps and liquefy the roof.

The ceramics factory closed in 1969. The cheese factory closed in 1970. The one restaurant, which had opened its doors in the twenties, stayed in business but with different owners. First it had been the Paris Restaurant, then Paris Home Cooking. Presently it was called Dolly's Diner. Like the restaurant, there was always a bank in the same location, but that too had changed names.

From the forties to the seventies a bus ran daily from New York City to Paris. It stopped in front of the hardware store and then went to Sharon and eventually on into Buffalo, but in 1978, when Route 17 was completed and people going downstate drove instead, the bus service stopped.

Next to the bank there always was and still is a driveway lined with cypress trees. They were planted in 1905 and by 1982 they were a tall and stately entrance to the cemetery. Among the gravestones, several names were prominent. The Baldwin, Paris, Swick, and Fenton families were in clear majority among the deceased. The descendants of Ebenezer Swick left the area in 1969 when they moved their ceramics factory to Ohio, but William's branch of the family had gone into the cattle business instead of pottery and they stayed. Nathan Swick bought the farm on Eastern Road, enlarging the house, repairing the barn, and managing the three hundred acres. When Nathan died, he passed the farm to his son,

William. William held an auction, and the animals, tractors, and all the farming equipment were sold. William used the money to buy books—rare books and used books—and then in 1949 he opened his bookstore in what used to be the old bakery.

Though the Fenton and Paris families died out, there were still Baldwins and Swicks in the phone book. Some of them occupied the old family houses, many of them divided into two or three residences, but some lived in the neighborhood that had been built on the east side of the village between the wars. Others occupied trailers scattered along the roads on the fringes of town.

Even the land and the streams and the forest changed. By 1982, the hundred and twenty-five dairy farms that had once flourished in the Paris countryside were all gone. Although many of the farmhouses were occupied, the barns were empty and the pastures weren't grazed on or cultivated. Still, at the high school, they had annual elections for the Dairy Princess, who reigned over the county fair. There was still a milk-processing plant in the town of Sharon, and in the county as a whole there were sixty-two working dairy farms (down from five hundred) and four of them, although not in the town of Paris, were in the Paris school district.

The soil that for two centuries had been the grazing land for animals was a mixture of clay and shale made even more inhospitable by the acid in the rain that blew into New York State from Ohio. Crop farming wasn't profitable so there were only small-scale truck farms and family vegetable gardens, which were dressed from year to year with healthy loads of lime and manure.

The most prosperous citizens in Paris had been the producers of milk and meat. And the manufacturers of ceramics and cheese. And the servers of law and hardware. The most prosperous in 1982 were the reapers. They were the men who cut away the hillsides for gravel and logged the forests for lumber. But the wealthiest were the reapers who dealt in trash. They were the enterprising individuals who contracted with waste-management companies from downstate to truck refuse into this distant northwestern corner. They dumped tires, rat poison, refrigerators leaking coolant, and all the assorted household detergents and paints and cleaners into a trench dug out of the land. When it was full, they sealed it over with topsoil and dug out a new one.

That bit of engineering satisfied the board of health and the Department of Environmental Conservation, but deep in the ground, nature kept everything moving. The rain seeped through the layers, doing its job, winding its way through plastic and metal, changing color and density as it mixed in with the chemicals. It dropped further into the earth via the tunnels the earth provides and emptied into the aquifers that pool in the ground in places that are deeper and more hidden than anywhere the scientific mind has ever measured, and deep in the bowels of the land, a thick yellow effluent drained into the underground waterways.

Three

≈

*H*arry owned Better Days, a drinking establishment that had been a part of his life for thirty years. He smoked too much, drank too much, and called going for a drive exercising. He figured that his years as a wrestler, before he started tending bar, had conditioned his body in a way that was everlasting. Under his drooping belly the solid muscles he once had were still there, just relaxed, waiting for a chance to stiffen up and take control. That was an opinion he didn't voice out loud. What he did was his own business and likewise with what he believed. But just to prove it to himself, he made twice-yearly visits to the gym in Sharon and, so far, he hadn't embarrassed himself.

Harry's apartment was above the bar in rooms that reeked not only of the cigarettes he smoked, but of the beery odor that rose up through the heating ducts from downstairs. Most of his furniture had come from a close-out sale at an office-supply warehouse ten years ago. The table and chairs and couch, all metal with imitation leather upholstery, were solid, practical pieces that would never wear out. The only item of beauty he had allowed himself to buy when he first moved in was the queen-size bed that took up most of the back room. The bedspread was made of rabbit pelts. It smelled of sex because he liked to roll around on it with whoever was his current woman, but like the beer smell, it was something a person got used to.

On Wednesday evening, Harry was in the tub. Helene was coming with sandwiches, as usual on Wednesday night. His friend Jack was serving downstairs and all Harry had to do was go in tomorrow morning to count the cash and check supplies. When he heard her coming up the stairs, he kicked the door open without leaving the bath and called, "In here!" There was rustling in the kitchen. He heard the scuttle of her shoes hitting the floor. "Come 'ere! I'm in the tub!"

"Finish up!" she called. "I'll see you when you're decent!"

He thought of all the indecent things they had done together and said, "You're a funny woman."

"Ha, ha!" she answered.

"Get me a beer then."

"Get a beer yourself."

Why couldn't the woman just do what you wanted her to do? With his toes he pulled out the plug. Then he stood up and passed a towel over his big soft body. His hair was curly and after toweling it, he ran his fingers through to give it a comb. He stepped out of the tub onto the dry mat and stood in front of the sink, cleaning out his fingernails. Then he sat on the side of the tub and pulled on a pair of clean pants and a T-shirt. They were fragrant and too tight from the laundry. He took a towel and dried between his toes. Then he sprinkled talcum powder and rubbed it into his feet. He walked barefoot to the living room. Helene was sitting on the couch, staring straight in front of her. Her eyelids looked heavy; her face was slack with tiredness. But Harry didn't notice those things. What he saw instead was the solid shape of her bottom. He knew the softness her navy postal uniform pants concealed. "You're not happy," he said, sitting down next to her.

"I am happy. Just this afternoon I was thinking that I am. Have you seen how beautiful it is in the country? The leaves are almost all fallen off and the trees are so old and naked."

"I went for a drive yesterday morning."

"On a drive you see nothing."

When she turned to look at him, he followed the line of her neck as it plunged into her shirt collar and met her bosom, which looked large and official in her postal uniform blouse. He wanted to free her, let all of her shapes fall loose into his hands. On her face he saw the land where she lived. The ragged pastures with their broken fence lines sat on her flat wide cheeks scorning a man who admired scenery from behind the windshield of his car. "Yeah, well, each to his own." He took her hand. "Hey sweetheart, you're looking good."

"After sandwiches. I'm hungry."

"And I'm thirsty."

She pointed to the refrigerator and he went over and got what he wanted.

"A letter came today from Gunter."

"Oh yeah, what's your brother up to?"

"What he's up to I don't know. Monday is the day of the death of our mother and he was writing to me because of it."

"That's nice of him."

"I like it," she said simply.

Harry hadn't known Helene's mother. Even though it was a small town, he wasn't sure that he had ever seen her. All he could call to mind was the snapshot in the newspaper that showed a pale timid face peeking out from under a fringe of hair. What he knew about her was only what the obituary had said. Uta Hugel had come to America from Germany with her two small children and met William Swick, used book merchant. The accident wasn't her fault. It was some old fart, about ninety years old, who had caused it. He'd strayed out of his lane coming up to the rise and collided with her right on her own road, just a mile from the farmhouse where she lived. Harry'd driven by it once and he knew it was a drafty, tumbledown place because Helene dressed in more clothing than any woman he'd ever been with.

"You and Gunter got along good?" he asked her. He had known her brother before meeting her. Not well—he was one of those professional health freaks, the kind of guy who trained for the hell of it, jogging, watching his diet, staying off sex. The kind of guy who liked to have a woman for a friend. They'd talked down at the pool a few times. That was when Harry used to swim twice a week, before he understood his body's eternal conditioning. Gunter came in at the same time to do more laps than he cared to know about.

"Of course not," Helene said. "We are brother and sister. We always fought. Our mother always yelled at us to stop. We became friends when we grew up. You have a sibling?"

"Five," Harry said, but he didn't want to talk about them. "Can I get you a beer?" he asked, going for his second.

"No, let's eat."

He took down the plates and she unwrapped the sandwiches. They were huge, thick slices of bread dripping with mustard and sauerkraut. Helene was one of the few women he'd been with who didn't try to starve herself. She sat on the couch with the butcher paper from the sandwich spread across her lap and the plate on top of it. She ate slowly, but never more slowly than he did. He ate breakfast and lunch, but his dinner he drank. His sandwich lay untouched on the table.

"I've been scattering seeds," Helene said.

"Seeds? What kind of seeds?"

"All kinds. Milkweed, mullein, joe-pye weed."

"What're them?"

"All beautiful wildflowers that I want to grow around the house."

"What about the lawn?"

"We got rid of it. When Gunter left, we stopped mowing. Every morning I go out into the fields and collect seeds in a little bag and when the bag's full, I bring it home and scatter. It's how you spread the news to the wildflowers that they have more room."

"That's nice," he said, wondering how Harold Neil Dunbar ever got hooked up with a woman who wanted weeds in her yard.

"'Lovely milkweeds!' I say. 'Beautiful and tall joe-pye!' You see, I talk to them. I show them where there is a little stream and put the seeds down next to it because that's what the joe-pye likes. 'Oh sweet and everlasting bird's-foot trefoil that grows in dry sandy soil and blooms all summer long, you will like it here.' That's what I say. I throw those seeds along the driveway."

"You are one crazy woman!"

"'May you spread and be healthy,' I say as I throw out the seeds. I picture the field around the house in July with so many loosestrife it will be all purple. It is very good to live where the plants grow. Did you know that?" She looked at him so seriously that he laughed.

"I don't miss that green stuff one iota."

"So what do you see?" she asked.

He was going to blow it off with a wisecrack, but she stopped him with her eyes. "Whadya mean?"

"When you look out your window, what do you see?"

"Hell, I don't know. The goddamn street."

"May I teach you something?" She put her sandwich down and stood up.

"Sure, teach me anything." He held his arms out for her, but she said, "Come here. Put down your beer and come to the window. Now tell me something interesting that you see."

He walked over and looked out. It was the same Main Street as always. "Just the buildings."

"No. There isn't just the buildings. There is something. There is something beautiful and unexpected across the street."

"You know that for a fact?"

"Always. You look till you see it."

It was getting dark. The cars had their headlights on. The hardware store was dark. The lawyer's office was dark. The bank was dark but the time and temperature flashed stupidly. People were going in and out of Smokes and Jokes. Some of them he knew. Two of them were women he had fucked. Eventually, in a town this size, he could sample every woman between twenty-five and fifty. Should he make it his goal? Possibly. Helene shifted her weight behind him. She never wore perfume but her body had a fragrance he associated with something out there: wind or cold or night. It called to him and he stumbled after it every time, but never got all that he wanted.

"Well?"

"It's getting late. Let's try this in the daytime."

"No, you keep looking."

He looked out his window to the windows across the street. The fact was he had once been in one of those rooms above the stores. They were attics, never used for much of anything. A lot of wasted space. Someone once told him it was the building codes that made the Main Streets of American towns so vacant. Something about not mixing business with residential. His own apartment was illegal. But in ten years, no one official had bothered him. At night, when the bar was closed, the street was his private domain and he walked in front of his windows without bothering to pull down the shades. "You're going to be disappointed. I don't see nothing."

"Then do something. Pretend that you're seeing it all for the first time. You've never been up here and you're looking out. You've gone into the shops across the street a million times before, but you've never looked to see what was above them."

"All right, all right, I see something. Come in closer."

She stood behind him and peered over his shoulder. Across the way, there was a light on in the room upstairs. At that very moment, a man walked across the empty floor. They could see him clearly. He was young, had loose clothing, longish hair. Then a woman in a dress joined him and the light went off. A teenager and his girlfriend. They had the right idea. He maneuvered Helene in front of him and put his hand on her large ungirdled behind.

She removed it. "Later. Not until after the interesting thing."

He put his hand on her waist and said, "Well, I've never seen a light go on across the way. I assumed the upstairs of those buildings wasn't wired. They're always dark."

"See, you take the time to look and the world will come to you." She saw William cross the street with his dog, Buster. He went into Smokes while Buster stayed out on the sidewalk.

"Yeah, the world comes," Harry said. He put his other hand on her belly and felt her heat rise.

"Not yet." She watched William appear and walk around to the alley. "Tell me what they were doing there."

"They're high school kids looking for a place to make out."

"You're so sure of that? I am not so convinced." She walked out of his embrace and into the kitchen.

"What does what a couple of kids are doing matter to us? C'mere!"

"No. You stay there. I stay here at the table. Now, tell me why it was interesting."

He liked to have a woman every seven days. If you didn't keep it working, what would stop it from shriveling up? "I'll tell you what was so interesting and then you'll come over here to the couch."

"When I'm ready."

"It's not interesting. A light went on in a room over the newspaper store and we saw a man and a woman. What could be interesting there?"

"Tell me more."

"Hell, I don't know. I've lived here, what, ten years, and I've never seen that light before. That's something. Now come on and sit over here on my lap."

"Tell me more."

"Two people. A boy, maybe eighteen, it's hard to tell with a street between us. Let's say eighteen. He walks across a room, which is empty. What could I see? Not much. Cardboard boxes maybe. Empty walls. A woman appears. Young too, probably the same age. She's not dressed in jeans like he is. She's got on a red dress."

"Long?"

"Long. And out goes the light. That's what I saw. Now c'mere, you big beautiful woman. Come and sit on my lap."

"What did she look like?"

"Lots of dark hair. Hanging down. She looked like a Gypsy. The kind of girl a kid like that would want to be with. C'mere, you big beautiful lady."

"I come. But look at me, Harry."

He looked. There were the ragged fields. Her nose was the long grasses, her eyes pools of water, her mouth a river you could stand in. She knelt over him so close he could smell the smell between her legs.

"My face is pale and plain, yes? Ordinary. I have thick eyebrows, a thin mouth, eyes wide apart. Not beautiful, Harry. Again, tell me what I'm like."

He put his face in her bosom and mumbled, "School's over, sweetheart."

"Do you want me to sit next to you?"

"You big woman, you c'mere. C'mere, sit on your old Harry's lap. Thatta girl. You're a big, plain-looking ugly woman. Okay? Now, sit down." He reached up and turned off the light and in the shadowy room his hands went to all of the buttons, zippers, and hooks on her clothing and slowly he peeled it away.

Four

~~~

William Swick hadn't felt right since they took out his spleen. It wasn't that he missed the organ; his body had adjusted quickly and all systems seemed to be working well, but he felt as though his insides weren't in quite the right places. They'd been pushed around. And yet he knew from his research that a splenectomy was not a complicated procedure. It was simply a matter of clamping the pedicle.

But doctors were busybodies. And with the excuse of exploratory surgery, they must have poked and prodded and pressed at all his organs. He was certain they'd seen right away that the spleen needed to be removed but they couldn't restrain themselves from a little extra investigation. It was their training; they'd spent years cutting up rats and dogs in medical school and to them a body was a thing splayed open and ready to be looked at. They had no respect for the privacy of the individual system. So when he was on the operating table with all his insides staring up at them, they took advantage of the situation. Not for medical reasons, but simply to gawk. When the sideshow was over, they'd tumbled it all back in too haphazardly. Maybe they'd been playing too long and were called to another operation. So maybe the intern threw it all back in and stitched him up. The result was that his body wasn't his any longer. It wasn't home.

That was just the feeling his father had warned him about. But public school cruelties were nothing compared to the fear that his guts had been tampered with. Those mornings, sitting on his father's lap before the school bus came to pick him up, couldn't have prepared him for the deep physical suspicion that was in his body now. It was far more insidious because he couldn't accuse them. He couldn't demand that they open him up and put him back right. Then they surely would laugh behind his back. He would simply have to accept this indignity as he had learned to accept the others.

"Are you my boy?" his father would say to him on those dark winter mornings. His father was a big rough deep-spoken man. He had his own beliefs. When the DEC came to test the water in their well for contaminants his father sent them off the property. But not before they saw ten-year-old William playing in his yard.

"Birth defects can be caused by pollution," the man with the briefcase said as his father marched them towards their car.

It wasn't even true for William, whose height was determined by genetics.

"No birth defects around here. I got a herd of healthy cattle and a healthy son."

"Have it your way. But if you got a problem we should be notified so we can identify the source."

On school mornings William sat on his father's lap from six in the morning until seven when the bus pulled up in front of their barn. When the blinking lights moved over the kitchen walls, they got up and walked outside. The driver was already standing by the stairs, ready to help him up. He was the only student who needed help onto the bus. There weren't any other dwarfs of any age in the entire county and now there wouldn't ever be dwarfs again because the busybody doctors had done so much poking around they had figured out how to screen fetuses for normalcy. Now, only those babies who were a standard size were helped into the world.

He slid down from his stool and lowered the shade on the front door of the shop. It was his own Hell. When people met him for the first time he was repulsive to them or else he was interesting. They wanted to run away or they wanted to take his picture. What a gift it would be if he could walk through the world simply, with the same expectation of being received as other people.

There had been a lot of traffic in and out of the store during the day and now there was a stack of books that needed reshelving. He pulled the ladder over to fiction. Once he climbed up it, he could move from one location to another along the overhead track without ever having to climb down. Kids liked to come in and play on his invention but they were too rough with it and once a particularly determined little boy had loosened the wheels. He screwed them in more securely after that and made a playroom in the children's section to keep them away from the rest of the store. Buster installed himself there. They could pull his ears or climb on his body and he wouldn't flinch. It was unusual for an old dog to put up with such indignities, but Buster was exemplary. His other saint-like quality was the control he had over his bladder. By the time the books were reshelved, the day's intake recorded, the dog had moved up to the front door to make his needs clear. William let him out and returned to pack his briefcase.

The most interesting book to come in all day was a volume published in 1938 called *Solitary Hours.* He hadn't had time to look at it, but a first glance told him it was a book of poetry that wouldn't go in the poetry section but on the oddities shelf where he kept all the most curious publications. There was Dr. Gilmour's *Recipe for Healthy Lungs,* which included photographs of the author in an exercise suit doing push-ups. And Karen Cornfield's *Confessions of a Sunday School Teacher,* which was an agonized testament chronicling her recurring doubts about the existence of God. William put the book in his briefcase, stepped down off the platform behind his desk, and reached up to turn off the fluorescent. The light from the street bathed the store in a bluish glow. He locked the door while Buster finished his business and then the two of them proceeded down the sidewalk.

Being short, William looked up at the skyline, which everyone who was tall took for granted. At this time of year, the sun would set just over the rooftops and he would see gaudy displays that most other people missed. Tonight, for instance, the sky was streaked with pink. He stopped in front of the bar to watch it. Yellow light simmered over the roofs with a splash of green at the top. Purple moved into pink and grew deeper, harder, edging the pink out. He could see the gray clouds descending as a light flicked on in one of the second-story windows. He didn't think anyone ever used the rooms up there and he stared at the silhouette of a man and a woman against the window. The woman walked away and William lost interest and crossed the street. Leaving Buster on the sidewalk, he went into Smokes and Jokes for his paper. Then both of them walked around behind the store to his parking spot. Buster climbed into the back of the pickup and he climbed in the front.

Once home, Buster sniffed around outside the house to see what animals had been there. William went into the kitchen and started dinner. He sliced two tomatoes that had been ripening on the windowsill, grated a purple onion, and opened a can of sardines. That and two pieces of the bread Uta used to have shipped from Buffalo, a practice he continued, was his customary fare Wednesday nights when Helene worked late at the post office. He set the book up next to his plate, sat down, and started to read. The pages were yellowed and musty. He turned to a single short rhyming poem opposite an illustration. The illustrations were the simple line drawings popular at the time and were quite nice, but the poems were awful.

Solitary hours
During the long life spent
Makes the heart grow sad
And the soul lament

They were authored by a Miss Eloise Baldwin, a name he was familiar with. She probably paid for the printing out of her own pocket. Well, he hoped she had achieved some satisfaction. It was a handsome volume and would make a nice birthday present for someone with insipid taste.

September month of sunny days
Calls forth October when frost o'er the valley lays

He turned to the front page to find the publisher and discovered that the book had been published ten miles away in Sharon, New York. Before the second world war, in every sizable town there had been a small press, ready to publish the outpourings of local residents. Eloise Baldwin had lived in Paris. She was from the family that owned the department store.

William climbed down to get some mustard out of the refrigerator, which he mixed in with the sardines. Then he piled the mash onto the bread. He chewed slowly, watching the light in the kitchen deepen. It was dark by the time he finished. Then he opened another can of sardines and mixed them in with Buster's food.

Uta would not have approved. When she was alive, Buster lived outside and ate nothing but dog food. It was his place in the natural order and if nothing else, Uta was a woman who knew where things belonged. Not only animals, but the dishes in a cupboard and the furniture in a room. She also knew how pleasure fit into a life of work.

Every few days he made love to her. It was something he had never been able to do before, not because of physical problems, but simply because he didn't know any small women and assumed that the tall ones wouldn't be interested. It took someone in desperate circumstances, like a woman who spoke little English and had only two small children, two suitcases, and the address of a relative who must have changed his mind as soon as they wrote and told him they were coming, a woman who was ready to find a home any way she could, to offer him a chance to act on his fantasies. If Uta were alive those doctors wouldn't have played around with his guts. She would have stood her full five feet and demanded they treat him like anyone else. She was also the one who instructed him to eat sardines for calcium and organ meat for iron to keep up his stamina. She didn't approve of the chickens wrapped in plastic at the supermarket. She wanted a butcher. Not finding one, she fixed up the old chicken shed and asked him to get her day-old chicks, which he did soon enough simply by going to the feed store. They started them in a box in the kitchen and as they grew, so did his fondness for this woman who had entered all the dark corners of his existence. The next spring when the hens didn't sit on their eggs, she made lids to cover their nesting boxes and trapped them in there for as long as it took to teach them the maternal responsibility that had been bred out of their genes. The chickens outside now were the progeny of those first hens. They gave them eggs and chicks and meat. He realized that it was in that way, the way she had made everything function, that her absence sometimes was the most painful. He envied her son, Gunter, who could get into his car and drive away from it all.

Five

Helene didn't like to stay overnight at Harry's because she'd arrive at the post office smelling of cigarettes. Even if she left right after showering and changed into fresh clothes, she could smell tobacco on her skin all day long. But she had stayed last night because they'd made a deal. If he wanted her to come again he had to wake up early in the morning with her and find something out of the window to talk about. The sight of Harry with his eyes open at seven o'clock was worth cigarette stink.

The rain began with a clap of thunder just as she got out of bed. Water pounded on her back in the shower as it pounded on the roof outside. The gutters rang, and the dusty windows in Harry's living room turned brilliant under the downpour. He stood in front of one now, scratching his belly, wearing nothing but shorts. "Hell if I know. Window's open over there. The same one was lit up last night. Those kids left it open and water's getting inside."

"Come here, have your coffee, tell me about it."

"I already told you all there is to know. The fucking window's open." He straddled the chair across from her and added, "And you're a wild woman."

Maybe she was. She knew that the way he made her feel came from his simple, unapologetic obsession with sex. But this morning she was satiated and she didn't want to be touched or teased or in any way worked up. "Why do you think the window's open? What were they doing?"

"Smoking pot. They wanted ventilation."

"But why'd they go up there to smoke pot? It would have been easier to do it outdoors. It wasn't that cold last night. There's woods all around."

"Hell if I know."

"Imagine it."

"Maybe they wanted to screw too. She didn't want to lie down in the grass. Too buggy."

"You always think with your cock, don't you?"

"Listen, sweetheart, it's too early, I'm going back to bed."

"Well then, I might have to find myself another boyfriend." She wondered if that would be possible. Her body had come to expect its once-a-week release on his filthy rabbit pelts. Who else would be able to figure her out as quickly as he had? That was what she had sensed the first night he served her a drink in his bar: that in some inexplicable way he knew her better than anyone else.

"Don't try to make me your intellectual. Because my brain went to sleep a long time ago."

"There's nothing intellectual about this. It's just keeping your eyes open. It's living in the world, Harry."

"You're trying to reform me."

She stood up and grabbed her pocketbook. "And what have you done to me? I know every inch of your body and what am I going to do with it? I can't move in with you. I can barely stand to come over here one night a week. It's just an exchange. That's all. I'm trying to give you something that I know."

"I love you."

"Don't be crazy. I could be anyone, it doesn't matter. You love women. And I'm trying to show you there's something else out there.

"Also..." She came around to his chair, touched his soft curly hair. "I'm forty-one. Maybe I don't want to grow up to be an old maid."

"You talking marriage or some nonsense like that? Wake up, Helene. Open your eyes. I'm an old fart. I don't believe in monogamy, much less marriage."

"I'm not talking marriage, Harry. I'm saying that I was brought up without a father. My baby would be, too."

"You're pregnant?"

"No, I'm not pregnant. But maybe I want to be. Maybe it's time."

He patted the chair next to him. "Sit down, sweetheart. Put down your pocketbook."

"No thank you."

"No babies. I got an allergy to them. They stink. They make noise. I can't stand them. The world's going to have to continue without Harry's addition to the gene pool. And it's my loss, I know it. But it's one of the rules of my existence."

"Then you shouldn't make love to women."

"I should. I should have that pleasure always but I had the tube rerouted."

"You had a vasectomy? Then how come you use a condom?"

"Double protection. Keeps old Harry safe. What would you do with a kid anyway? What the hell kind of a life would that be?"

He stroked her leg. She felt the heat of his hand through her uniform. "I don't really know."

"Well, it would complicate everything. And for what reason? To satisfy some primitive urge? Some outdated desire to procreate? Think about it."

"I'm interested in possibility. That's all. I want to move out, expand. I don't want to live in a narrow little room. This is a narrow little room you've made for yourself, Harry. It's too cut off. The air is stuffy. I don't want to live like you do. I have to make other choices. So maybe a baby, but then I am old and maybe you're right, maybe it's not really the answer. I don't know. But somehow, there needs to be more movement in here, at least for me. There need to be ideas and feelings."

"Did I ask for a critique of my lifestyle? No, I did not."

"One friend to another friend, that's all this is. I'm making observations, thinking out loud, saying how I am different. Now, do you want to hear why I think the window was open?"

"You're wet. I smell you. Don't go to work this morning. Call in sick."

"Get your hand off me!" She took a step backwards. She should leave and that would be the end of it. But then maybe she should give him one more chance. "Listen to me and listen to me good because if we can't do this together we can't continue. Now, I'm going to tell you why I think the window was open. You can think about it, then I'll stop in after work and see if you have anything to add. Okay? Are you going to listen? Okay, they're friends, they're not lovers. He's even a virgin. He's very studious and good at sports and comes from a family that cares about him. And buys him enough clothes and is planning to send him to college. See that word on the building over there? Did you notice it?"

He followed her to the window and through the rain saw the words that stood out in relief across the red tile at the top of the building across the street. *Baldwin Mercantile.* Funny how he'd never seen it.

"Maybe his last name is Baldwin and let's say that his great-grandfather built that building to expand their dry-goods business into a department store. Let's say that when he was a child he used to go there and he remembers the children's department and how it was up on the second floor. He knows the back stairway and happened to discover sometime ago that the owner of Smokes and Jokes never kept it locked."

"Funny that in all those years I never made out the words over there."

"But what were they doing? Why did those two kids have the light on last night? I don't know. That's for you to tell me when I get back."

Harry returned to bed after she left. He had to store energy for the next morning when he wouldn't get to sleep till three A.M. All traces of the rain had disappeared by the time he woke up again and the first thing he did, even before reaching for his cigarettes, was look out to the window across the street. It was still open, and right above it, in tall block letters that were less obvious now that they had dried, were the words Baldwin Mercantile. The roof peaked just above them, the line of the angle formed by bricks laid up like stairs. A pigeon sat over the M in Mercantile.

Harry moved to the kitchen and had another cup of coffee and ate a doughnut he discovered in the box sitting on the counter from yesterday. He showered, shaved, dressed, and was already down on the street before he realized what he was about to do. But he canceled that intention and went into the newspaper store to buy his next carton of cigarettes and a paper. He didn't even look at the headlines, just folded it under his arm, walked to the end of the block, and turned into the alley that ran behind the stores that faced Main Street. Baldwin Mercantile was the third one in from the end. A sign on the back door of Smokes and Jokes said AUTHORIZED PERSONNEL ONLY. It was a metal door that looked like it had been bashed in too many times by the garbage truck. And indeed the Dumpster stood right next to it. Next to the Dumpster there was another door, a wooden one without a sign. He turned the handle, expecting it to be locked. But it turned easily. He was going to tug on it a little to pull it open when something inside of him said, "Wait a minute, what's going on here?" What *was* going on? He pulled it open and found himself looking up a set of narrow stairs.

Six

~~~

At the post office Helene discovered that a family named Baldwin lived in town. The names listed at their address were Robert Baldwin, M.D., Patricia, Darryl, and Emily. They lived in what was jokingly referred to as the suburbs of Paris, the ten blocks of modern residences built on the east side. Though she had never seen their house, she pictured the neat lawn and flowerbeds. They would be the type of family that traveled on all their vacations. They'd go to San Francisco, Orlando, Montreal, cities she'd never been to. They were the kind of people who wanted to show their children that other places were not as racially isolated or economically depressed or culturally deprived as Paris, New York. She imagined what the mother and the doctor father looked like. They used the East Paris post office so she didn't know them.

As she sorted the mail and waited on customers she thought about the kids she had seen through the window last night. He was dark and thin. He wore a plaid, button-down shirt that hung out of his pants, suggesting a disregard for clothing. Yes, she was starting to get a feeling for what he was like. A quiet, intense kid who didn't do well in school but was very quick and smart at anything that wasn't academic. He could fix engines and sewing machines and bicycles. Somehow, he just knew how things were put together. He could paint. He was working on a series of large oil paintings. They were fantastic landscapes, rich and colorful, of the hillsides, gorges, the trees he saw around there.

Helene had worked at the post office so long that the process of sorting, stamping, and weighing was automatic. All postal issues had a solution, so her job was easy and let her relax enough to invent mysteries in the rest of her life. That she wasn't satisfied with simply being a mail clerk and lived more happily in her imagination was a condition she blamed on her mother. Uta had rarely followed the rules.

At twelve-thirty, she called up Uncle William and asked him if he'd like some company for lunch. When she went outside, the clock on the bank, which was always five minutes slower than the clock at the post office, said 12:25. The temperature was forty-nine degrees. There was a light breeze that carried an autumn chill. She buttoned her jacket. Then she stopped at the restaurant to buy William the hamburger he would have walked over to buy for himself, and purchased a few pieces of fruit at the grocery for her own lunch.

William waved from the ladder where he was reshelving books. Buster walked down from the children's area to greet her. He was too old to jump up on her anymore, so he simply wagged his tail and pushed his nose into her skirt. She set their lunches on the desk and pulled up the rocking chair for William and a straight-backed chair for herself. She never explained where she spent Wednesday night and he would never ask. She supposed that, having a business in the center of town and being the kind of man people liked to chat with, somebody would have told him. He would wonder why she spent her time with an uneducated bartender who was old enough to be her father, but he would figure that it was her business. She poured them each a cup of tea. Then she sliced her fruit and laid it on her plate with a few crackers.

"You're just like your mother," William said, noticing her plate as he sat down.

"It's a habit you learn in a country where they don't have perfect apples. If you slice them, chances are you'll find the worm." She said it cheerfully, choosing not to notice that William's eyes were shiny. They both knew worms weren't the only reason for Uta's apple etiquette. She always cut her fruit and sliced her cheese because she did things in a careful way. When she sat down to eat, she placed all of her food on the plate neatly and then slowly, methodically ate her way through it. She had done everything in that thoughtful manner except die. That had been huge and sudden and messy and the person it must have shocked most of all was Uta herself.

William pulled a book out of his briefcase and slid it on the desk toward her.

"What's this?" she asked, picking up the blue clothbound volume. When she opened it to the title page and read *Solitary Hours* in beautiful lettering and Eloise Baldwin below it, she was amazed at the synchronicity. She wanted to ask a dozen questions. William had grown up in the same house he now lived in. He had walked down the same Main Street as a child with parents who had walked down it with their parents. Perhaps he had even known the Baldwins. Perhaps his mother used to buy his clothes at Baldwin Mercantile. She envied such a solid, unremarkable past.

She had been born in Germany and grew up in Dresden, close to a park where there were statues and fountains and topiaries. After the war, her mother had moved them to the British occupied zone of Germany and they'd lived with other refugees in crowded settlements. That was where Gunter was born. It was no wonder Uta had followed any lead to get to America. A letter from someone distantly related and living in New York State was enough to make her save her money till she could pay for passage on a freighter. Poor Uta, taking the bus to Paris to walk down an empty Main Street, past plain two-story buildings that had been standing for only a century. What did she do with her own rich past with its baroque palaces and museums that had taken decades to build and only one absurd night to destroy?

"Is this Baldwin someone you know about?"

"The family was known. They ran a department store, Baldwin Mercantile; it probably was in business for about fifty years. They're still around here, but they're not in the clothes business anymore, which is a shame. My mother used to buy everything there because they had a tailor for alterations. In those days, no one expected store-bought clothes to fit you. So I wasn't the only one who had to have them altered. It always seemed like such a huge place. I remember how the wooden floors creaked every step you took. The saleswomen were such gossips, they knew who was getting married, who was having babies, which women's husbands brought the paycheck home and which ones drank half of it away before the wife could get her hands on it. At Christmas, they'd put up a huge evergreen tree. One time it was so tall they had to cut a hole through to the second floor. Nobody thought about the tree, of course, and what a waste it was to chop down such a magnificent specimen. That tree had been alive for some thirty years and they cut it down to bring it indoors for two weeks. We're an arrogant people, Helene. No respect."

"What about that hamburger you're eating there, William?"

He looked at it. "Ugly stuff, isn't it? I wish I didn't need meat, I wish I could just eat beans and rice."

"These Baldwins—why did they get rid of their department store?"

"They didn't. Bernie Baldwin inherited the store from his father and he was an idiot. He bought too many houses, had a mistress, ran up debt. By the time a department store opened up in Sharon people had cars, and he didn't have the stock any longer to compete."

"So what happened?"

"He went to Florida. Lived on income from rental properties up here and even those he didn't manage well. One burned down. Well, the Mercantile stood empty for a long time and then it was a ladies' dress shop and then Smokes and Jokes."

"So is Bernie Baldwin still alive?"

"That I don't know. Probably not. But he had a son. I don't know what ever happened to him, though."

"This Eloise Baldwin, would she have been an aunt or a sister of Bernie's?"

He thought about it for a while and then said, "I think she was his sister. Which fits. Neither of them had any creativity. Go ahead. Take a look at the poems."

Helene didn't trust her judgment about poetry but she read several and thought they were pleasant.

Mystery stands
At the top of the stair
Never says excuse me
Never says Beware

She kept her opinion to herself, because she knew William didn't like anything that wasn't a challenge to his intellect. A mystery waiting at the top of the stairs clearly wasn't that, but it coincided with all the other things that had happened in the last day and a half, except, of course, the post office.

Seven

*T*here wasn't a banister and once the door closed it all went black. Listening to a slight pounding in his brain, Harry started to climb upwards. He wondered if there was a light switch but, feeling around, the walls on either side of him revealed nothing. He was thinking with his cock now, creeping deeper and deeper into a dark place. He wasn't scared. Only amazed at the lengths he would go for cunt. Not that hers was any better than anyone else's. If she didn't return, there were dozens of others. Maybe hundreds, if he counted the ones he'd already known. He had once tried to keep track, but he'd left the piece of paper in his cash register one night where Jack found it and discovered his wife's name in the number-one position. That was years ago. They'd since patched up their friendship and there was no one he'd trust more. Jack would say the same of him. He'd once trusted Harry alone in his apartment overnight with Martha, who was Jack's woman after the ex had left him, and Harry had behaved himself. But he never made lists anymore. The only place he kept a tally was in his head.

At the top of the stairs there was a door. He didn't see it, but he walked into the knob. Hoping it would be locked so he could go back home, he turned it gently. The door swung open.

The light! He wasn't prepared for it. There were six floor-to-ceiling windows at the end of a large room. The floor looked sound enough, although right in the center there was a hole with a railing around it. He peered over it and looked down at the ceiling of the store downstairs. On the wall there was a poster. When he walked over, he could see it was a painting of a room with a huge green apple filling it almost entirely. It had been tacked up recently because the edges weren't yellowed. The apple in the painting was smooth and perfectly round and by the way the shadowing was done, you could tell the artist knew what he was doing. Odd that someone with all that talent would want to paint something so meaningless.

He turned his back on it and put his hands in his pockets. The picture made him a little uncomfortable, as though it were a person laughing at him. Well, let it laugh, he was going to look around. There were some shelves and clothing racks and a few dusty cardboard boxes, exactly the kind of worthless clutter you would expect to find. He walked to the windows and looked across to his rooms, but the sun made the windows black and he couldn't see anything. He looked below. Somebody passed right under the window, probably coming out of Smokes and Jokes. You could spy on everyone from up here. At night, when the lights were on across the way, you could spy on him. Of course, that was if you wanted to engage in a royal waste of time. As for him, he had better things to do. Since he was there, he closed the window the kids had left open, noticing how the rain had soaked into the floor underneath it. When he turned around he caught the apple staring at him and then he saw a door on the side wall that was probably the upstairs bathroom. He'd always liked old-fashioned bathrooms and in his apartment hadn't even considered replacing the claw-foot tub or pedestal sink. The old stuff was better made, better plumbed. He walked over to the door, but it was locked. It was probably one of those 1920s bathrooms with octagonal black-and-white tiles going up the wall and a tiny wall sink. He liked bathrooms so much he'd once thought about going into plumbing. He even went so far as to take a course at night, but when they began to learn the parts of the toilet he dropped it. He was not destined for any job that involved shit. His girlfriend at the time, Marlene somebody or other, wanted to have a baby and since that too would fill his life with shit, he dropped her as well. If you didn't want shit in your life, you said no to puppies, babies, and plumbing. When a man stayed firm on that, he stayed safe.

He closed the door at the top of the stairs, and crept down to the bottom in darkness. But he stood at the bottom for a moment before opening the door just to let it sink in what a fool he was. What was he going to say if someone happened to be walking down the alley when he stepped out? How was the owner of the Better Days Tavern going to explain what he was doing there?

Eight

~

*I*t occurred to William that they were all trapped. Why hadn't he left Paris a long time ago? He could have opened a bookstore in Chicago and hosted readings and discussion groups. He could have sold both used and new books. Why hadn't he done that when he'd finished college and was still young?

It was a matter of a loan. You needed money to start a business and here, the president of the bank knew the Swick name. He knew William and William's father. He didn't laugh at the idea of a dwarf wanting to open a bookstore. He was trapped because this was the only place where he was taken seriously.

They why didn't Helene leave? Why hadn't she driven out to San Francisco with Gunter after Uta died? What was keeping her?

William asked himself this question while he was sitting at his desk in the store. Helene was a smart woman. She should have had a career or gotten married. Or she could be working at a post office in a big city and going to museums and operas and plays. She could have met a man and fallen in love and had children. But she had stayed here. Why had she done that?

William wondered if he, in any way, was responsible. Had she stayed because she thought she needed to take care of him? The idea sickened him. No matter what he did, tall people assumed he was weak and inadequate, even the girl he'd given shelter to and helped raise since she was ten years old. Why should she waste her life in this small town because of him? He would urge her to leave. It was his responsibility. She couldn't stay here because she was concerned for him.

He finished putting the figures in his ledger, noting that for the second week in a row he had sold just enough to cover his overhead. The only time the store did well was at Christmas. It was a terrible fact, but the majority of people didn't read anymore.

Helene had arrived home before him. He could see her on the front porch when he came into the kitchen. He put down his briefcase, fed Buster, and went out to see her.

She was sitting next to a pile of roots and berries. Uta had taught her how to identify herbs and through the summer and into the fall she gathered them and laid them out on screens in the attic to dry. She used them all through the winter, ministering to her own complaints and William's and those of people she knew in the village. It was her private drugstore. He stepped over her piles and sat down on the concrete step. She was laying hawthorn berries out on a screen and she looked up and said, "I was so lucky. There was a tree covered with haws right near the path. Look at how much I picked!" She pointed to a pile of what looked like tiny red apples.

He knew that she dried the berries because they were good for sore throats. A practical woman, thinking ahead. He looked down at the valley and up into the hills where she'd been gathering. Most of the leaves were off the trees and in the middle of the grays and browns there were patches of yellow where the tamaracks stood. In another month their needles would fall and then everything would be somber.

"Helene, there's something I've been thinking about. You should travel, find a nice city to settle in, enlarge your world."

"You want me to move out?"

"Well, it might be time for you to move on. You should see other places, meet new people. And I've been thinking I'd like to live here alone."

"You want me to rent a place in the village so you can have this house all to yourself?" Her voice was shaky; he could hear the tears at the edge of it. She put the berries down and when she looked at him, her face was scared.

"No, I don't, not really. The house is too big for just me. I was only thinking."

"Thinking what?"

"That you would rather live in a big city."

"This is my home. My mother brought me here."

"But that was a mistake. Your mother never intended to live here with me. It was a lucky coincidence. But now..."

"I'm not a blood relative so you are asking me to leave. I don't want to burden you, William, so all right, I'll find another place. But I have a question." She moved the berries around on the screen nervously and when she spoke again her voice trembled. "Are you intending to sell the house? I would have to tell you I think it's a mistake."

"No!" He fairly shouted it. "No! I don't want to sell the house. I said it all wrong. I wanted to give you an easy way out. I didn't want you to stay because you thought you had to take care of me. Or that you had to pay me back for giving your family a place to live. I didn't want you to stay here for the wrong reasons, Helene, only for yourself."

"I am not a person separate from all of those other things."

"You can be. That's what I want to tell you. You owe me nothing."

She moved the berries around on the screen again.

"You are as free as your brother. Gunter didn't feel any responsibility to me. He left. I wanted to tell you that you can do the same if that's your desire."

She winced in pain. A thorn on a hawthorn branch had stabbed her thumb. Blood welled up. William pulled a tissue out of his pocket. She gave him her hand as though she were a little girl and he pressed the tissue over the wound. He did it without thinking because all their years together had given him the right.

But she took her hand back. "It's not my desire," she said. "Gunter did not know herbs. He didn't want to know them. I walk out there"—she pointed with her chin to the valley— "and I am following my mother on one of our herb walks. I am hearing what she said to me. I know the plants. I talk to them. They know me. How can I leave?"

"You like being here?" William asked, looking at the sagging porch, the broken steps, the clapboard that needed painting.

"I never thought about being anywhere else."

"Even though it's all going to hell? Everyone who lives here struggles. There's no leisure, no culture. And in the winter, there's no sun."

"But there's land. I need the land."

"Helene, if you ever want to go, you don't need to take care of me. I want you to remember that. You owe me nothing. We're not blood relatives and you can forget me if that's what you need to do."

She looked up and in the low evening light he could see Uta's face behind hers. Uta had the same green eyes and grayish blond hair, the same wide cheeks.

"Go if you want," he said.

"But I don't want. I want to stay."

Nine

~~~

It had been raining all day. When she left the post office the air was cool and wet. Leaves had come down from the maple tree onto her windshield. She wiped them off, watched them flutter down to the parking lot. Every fall, as the lush canopy of summer disappeared, she felt critical and dissatisfied. She had come to expect it and she supposed it was the inventory she needed to take before winter. In terms of the season, it made sense. As the squirrels gathered nuts and the beavers stockpiled branches, she made whatever changes in her life were necessary. But it had gotten worse since her mother died. A simple internal housecleaning became a tendency to attack people around her. Uta had taken things as they came. She didn't examine; she didn't question; she simply moved. And she rarely complained. Helene wondered if that was her mother's way or if it was simply because she had been happy.

With Uta gone, a calming element was missing from her life.

And here she was, criticizing Harry. And, she supposed, it was the reason William had spoken to her on the porch the other night. In William's eyes, Helene didn't measure up. If it had been December, none of this would have been happening. But because it was fall, people were interfering in each other's lives.

On the drive home, she thought about food. Tomorrow she would take the chicken in the refrigerator and make her mother's chicken and cabbage soup, but tonight they were going to have something simple: spaghetti with the tomato sauce she'd made just a few weeks ago and frozen. A knockwurst for William, who liked to have some meat at every meal.

Once she left town and entered the valley, she could smell the damp leafy smell of the earth. Mist started to rise in the air. Clouds of moisture hung over the brown fields. She entered a stretch where a bank of fog had settled over the road. She drove inside it and when she couldn't see anything but whiteness all around her, she panicked and hit the brake. But then she told herself this was simply practice. Wherever you were and whatever you were doing, when the end of your life came, you couldn't get scared, you had to keep steady and move bravely into it.

Helene kept her foot on the accelerator and followed what she could see of the edge of the road. She was inside a cloud. The familiar landmarks had been rolled out of sight. Wisps of fog broke off and fluttered in front of her headlights, making her dizzy. She hoped there weren't any other cars on the road and, gripping the steering wheel with nervous hands, proceeded into nothingness.

Ten

~~~

$\mathcal{E}$very morning when Stella Doyle woke up and looked out her window at the sun sitting like a big orange yolk over the railroad embankment, she would remember that Darryl Baldwin was at that moment sliding out of bed at his own house. They had set their clocks so that he woke up at the same instant she did. His white arm turned off the alarm at the exact moment her brown arm reached out to hit the ringer. One all-white American boy and one half-Mexican girl, with skin darker than anyone else's.

Not that she didn't like her color. She could see that it was more functional. She didn't get pimples or sunburn. Embarrassment didn't color her face. But it also kept her unknown. It made her appear aloof and hidden when what she wanted most of all was to be on familiar terms like everyone else.

After he stepped out of bed, she pictured Darryl putting on

the same clothes he had taken off the night before. He was a boy who didn't pay attention to what he wore. If only she could be the T-shirt he pulled on over his head or the pants he zippered and snapped at his waist. To be next to that pale skin all day and breathe in the dampness of those freckles at the base of his neck! She would be a sock on his foot! She would even be a shoelace on his sneaker just for the pleasure of being pulled and twisted by his fingers. What luck to be the jacket that he put on as he came down the stairs or the knapsack he wore on his back as he walked to school. It would be far better to be any of those things that lived at his house with him and were on his person all day long than to be Stella, who lived fifteen blocks in the other direction and only saw him in the cafeteria and after school. The sock would never embarrass him. It didn't try to extend a miserably small wardrobe with obvious gimmicks like scarves or jewelry. It didn't show up at school without money for lunch or live in an unpainted house where the roof over the porch had fallen down. If she were his T-shirt she would beg him to wear her out. She would kiss his chest with all of her threads and try to rub up against his red hair when it brushed the collar. If she were his shoelace she would stay tied from morning till night, remembering the touch of his fingers, and at bedtime when he wanted to take his shoes off, she would be limp and obedient.

In his house, every room had carpeting. It was vacuumed so often there were furrows in it from the brushes on the machine. His mother, who had red hair too, passed in and out of the rooms in that house soundlessly. No one cursed or shouted or snored on the couch and there were expensive things in the refrigerator to snack on like fruit juice and cheese. No one was expected to drink water. In his house they drank milk. If they ate crackers at all, they weren't saltines.

What kind of girl would she have been if she had grown up in a household like his? Well, she probably wouldn't have her color skin. And she'd have lots of clothes. But with more clothes and less disappointments maybe she wouldn't have fallen in love with him. Maybe it was finding nothing in the house to eat when she came home from school, not even any peanut butter to spread on the lousy saltines, maybe it was that which kept her empty enough so that when she looked at him she felt in every cell in her body just how full and satisfied he would make her feel.

She had two pairs of jeans and three shirts: the rose, the plum, and the navy. She never wore the same one two days in a row and she dressed them up sometimes with a string of beads or a pin, junk jewelry that people had left around in public places that she had picked up. The rose was her favorite shirt and as she put it on she wondered if he had ever wished that he could be the clothes she wore. Not likely. Someone from a house with carpeting in every room and a cheese and lettuce sandwich for a snack after school wouldn't ever want to be the shirt on her body. He took it for granted. Wasn't his plan to give it up as soon as he graduated? He was going to move into an attic to live and have his studio in so he could paint in the daytime and at night work as a truck mechanic for his uncle. His conviction, which was what she loved the most about him (besides his red hair, his long fingers, his thin body, his careless way of dressing, and his wonderful smell), also scared her. If she had a father who would pay for medical school, she would have been inclined to put her desires on hold and give medical school a try. You'd never get to have the kind of thick smooth carpets they had in his house if you made a living by selling paintings and fixing trucks. He didn't understand the necessities. Crackers and water might keep you from starving, but they didn't feed anything else. When he came to her house and walked up the stairs to her bedroom, which happened to be on the third floor because her mother's clutter took up the whole second floor, she could tell what he was thinking. But the romance of having cardboard boxes to put your clothes in and sleeping on a couple of foam rubber pads wore off quickly.

She brushed out her long hair and ran down the steps hearing snores from her mother's bedroom. In the kitchen, dirty dishes. There were diet soda, low-fat cottage cheese, and white bread in the refrigerator. Her mother must have brought food home last night when she got off from work. Stella pulled out two slices of bread, and not finding any margarine, ate them plain.

Outside, the windshield of her mother's Cadillac was covered with frost. By the time she woke up it would be long gone. As Stella looked at the car, she didn't gloss over the things that were wrong with it, she stared at them hard: at the passenger door that was a different color because her mother once drove into a fire hydrant and crumpled the original one, at the missing hubcaps, the busted fenders and the spots of rust that dotted the sides. Darryl thought it was romantic to run out of gas in the middle of town at four in the afternoon because the gauge didn't work and her mother had estimated the mileage wrong. She'd driven into town in her slippers and bathrobe to pick up the mail and there she was, with school out and all of Stella's classmates congregating on Main Street and not a buck in her wallet to buy gas or get herself home.

She saw the silhouette of a girl in front of her. It was probably Rhoda. Stella called and when she caught up, she saw that Rhoda was wearing the beautiful new winter coat she had been bragging about yesterday. It was barely cold enough for a sweater, but she supposed she would do the same if she owned a coat that had cost more than a hundred dollars. Stella swallowed her envy, pushing her hands into the pouch of her old gray sweatshirt.

"Did you get your speech done?" Rhoda asked.

Stella clapped her hand over her mouth and said, "Shit, I forgot all about it."

"You're kidding. You're going first today, remember?"

"Well, help me think of something. What's yours on?"

"The Declaration of Independence and how it's relevant today. I was up until midnight with the encyclopedia."

"She's going to flunk me."

"You'll think of something. Just walk to school real slow. I'm going to run ahead, okay? Good luck."

Stella watched Rhoda's fuzzy red back disappear down the sidewalk. The Declaration of Independence and how it was relevant today. Oh God, she had the feeling once again that she would never make it. Did all of those syllables really add up to anything? Like political? Mrs. Cleveland wanted them to speak about a topic that was controversial, relevant, and politically stimulating. Animal rights, for instance, euthanasia, civil disobedience, topics that were far beyond her idiot mind. As Stella walked under the railroad bridge, a word floated into her brain. Home. That's what she wanted to talk about, a simple one-syllable fact. How could a girl who wanted to talk about home ever measure up? Maybe she could dress it up a bit, call it Domestic Tranquillity, and then talk about the five essential ways to achieve it. What could they be? Plenty of food in the refrigerator, although before that there had to be money. Except that even with money, sometimes there wasn't any food. What would number one be? A clear-thinking adult. For home to be home the adults had to be functional. But what was controversial about that? Well, look how the culture preached all the things that made people lose their cool, like drinking, making money, being thin. Those were the things people got hooked on, that made them forget how to take care of themselves, and that was what she wanted to talk about. Could she say something like, "Our economic health depends on a certain percentage of adults feeling less than normal because they don't measure up to all the images"? Maybe she should focus on one thing, like weight. Could she say something like, "Obesity and capitalism have a symbiotic relationship"? That sounded good. Lots of syllables. But then everyone would know. Except they knew already. How could you hide your fat mother standing on Main Street wearing her bathrobe and slippers and looking helplessly at her ancient pink car? And where did she go for help? Better Days, of course, because she knew Harry would lend her a buck. He even got the gas for her himself.

That morning the school building frightened her. She was about to do something she'd never done before in her life. Speaking in front of the class wasn't unusual. They wrote book reports once a month and had to stand up at the front of the room and read them, but in a book report, she could hide. She couldn't with this. She would be as transparent as any of those white faces staring back at her because they would know, from her opening line, that it wasn't their mothers she was talking about, it was her own.

Eleven

~

The first thing Helene thought of when she woke up that morning was the chicken sitting on the bottom shelf of the refrigerator. She would set it in the Crock-Pot, surround it with onions, rosemary, chopped celery, and cabbage. She'd pour in a quart of water, add a tablespoon of salt, and let it cook all day long. By the time she got back from the office it would be soup.

Tomorrow night she'd set the table for four: William, herself, William's friend Faith who taught at the high school, and Harry. Should she invite Harry? It would mean it would be all over town. She decided she didn't care. Harry would enjoy a nice dinner. But could the four of them find something to talk about?

She decided to stop at Harry's on her lunch break and then decide. Maybe once she saw him she wouldn't feel like inviting him at all. That would make it simple.

It had been so cold the night before there was frost on the grass. All traces of the fog had disappeared. She fed the chickens and came back in to have breakfast and start the soup. Cooking in the morning with sunlight in the kitchen, the sky out the window over the sink, and smells rising up from the stove was a pleasure. As she chopped herbs and peeled onions, she realized that it was her pleasure in the morning and the chicken and the vegetables that would make everything taste good. Plus the fact that this bird was the progeny of her mother's first chickens, which she had coaxed into sitting on their eggs that first spring they had lived here when she and Gunter often stayed home from school because they felt shy about trying to speak English. Every spring after that, the new hens, who had been hatched from eggs that had been warmed by a chicken's body instead of an electric lamp, had the instinct to sit eggs in the spring. This mother-sat and mother-raised chicken was an anomaly in 1982. Maybe it was the only truly natural chicken for miles.

Twelve

Organ meat make you strong, she said. Chicken heart, chicken liver, chicken gizzard fresh, cooked well in salt and onion broth, chopped, spread on rye bread makes this—she pointed to the area below his belly—wangle.

He didn't know if it was German or simply Uta, but wangle was the word that came to his mind if he thought about such matters at all.

Which he did all the time. Wasn't fifty-eight too old for that? He decided it was allowed him because he had been a virgin till he was twenty-seven. All of those years of longing, made more desperate by the maternal feelings he knew he inspired in women, had created a monster. That night, after he made love to a woman for the first time, he wept.

And who would have him now? Faith? No, she would be appalled. Would he have to be content wangling by himself for the rest of his life? Even Buster, with his farts and swaying geriatric belly, found a female every once in a while.

When he came down to the kitchen Helene was gone but the soup was cooking quietly in the Crock-Pot and the organ meat she had chopped up and turned into pâté was in a bowl on the counter. He cut two thick slices of rye bread and slathered it on, saving a few tablespoons for the dog. Carrying his plate, he went out the front door and sat down on the porch steps to eat it. The valley lay below him, washed in glorious light.

Thirteen

~⌒~

Stella stood at the front of the room and looked out at the tree in the school yard. The brown leaves were paper thin in the sunlight. Some had fallen to the ground but most hung from the tree, stiff and crinkled.

"The Five Essentials of Domestic Tranquillity." She wasn't sure if she had actually spoken. The fifteen faces stared at her blankly. Had they heard anything? When she read her book reports, she had never noticed what their faces looked like because she had never taken her eyes off her page. Now she saw how expressionless they were.

"Number one, clear-thinking adults; number two, enough money coming in; number three, sufficient warmth for comfort; number four, plentiful food in the house; and number five, occasional love. First, I want to explain what I mean by occasional love and then return to number one, clear-thinking adults because that and number four, food in the house, is my focus. I say occasional love because, as everyone knows, no one can love you all of the time. You do something wrong, like forgetting to turn off the water in the bathroom and the sink overflows and your mother gets back from work and finds water all over the floor and at that moment she doesn't love you. But there has to be, for domestic tranquillity, a time during the day when you have a feeling that somebody loves you. Okay." She had been looking at the clock on the opposite wall and now she looked at the teacher, who nodded at her encouragingly. Stella took a breath. Out the window, the tree was dark and solid.

"The first essential for domestic tranquillity is a clear-thinking adult. This is not as easy to..." She hesitated. To have, to keep, to insure? No, *get* was what she wanted. "This is not as easy to get. A clear-thinking adult in the home is every child's right, but many children are deprived in this area and have to suffer." She looked around at all of the faces. Some looked amused, some interested, some bored. She refused to notice the bored ones and focused on a girl named Martha who was probably going to go to college on a scholarship because she was brilliant and poor. "Our culture preaches beauty. In the ads, being beautiful is associated with good times, financial success, popularity. But only thin people can be beautiful. We all know that. It's obvious. So the first requirement for being beautiful is to be thin. There is a lot of money spent in the process of getting thin, and walking through a supermarket you will be able to see how much it is on our minds. There is diet everything, from diet soda to eggs that don't have any cholesterol. In the drugstores there's pills for losing weight. In the magazines, clothing stores, movies, on TV, there are constant reminders of the need to be thin."

The faces in front of her were frightening so she looked out at the tree. "The problem is that we are a country of many different cultures and each of them has its own body type. Just to consider women for a minute. Oriental women tend to be thin. It's their body type. Irish women tend to be plump. It's not because they eat more than Oriental women, it's because that's the type of body they have."

Mrs. Cleveland had taught them the technique of punctuating their speeches with questions. Stella decided to try one. "If our culture teaches us that beautiful is successful and that thin is beautiful, what does the woman do who isn't thin?" She pictured her mother sitting at the kitchen table with an empty bottle of soda in front of her and a cigarette going in the ashtray. "She doesn't eat. But she gets so hungry she has to eat finally and when she does she feels guilty. That makes her eat even more and then she has to do everything she can to hide the fact that she's been eating too much. Food becomes an obsession. It blocks out everything else. This obsession makes clear thinking impossible.

"Who is responsible for what our image of beauty is? The food companies, the makeup companies, the drug companies. Even though we're a mixture of cultures in this country, which means we're a mixture of body types and skin colors, we are taught that only one type of body is beautiful, only one color of skin is beautiful. That's because a lot of money gets spent when people are dissatisfied. The people who don't fit the image buy diet foods, they buy hair colors, skin bleaches, girdles, exercise equipment. They will buy anything that promises to help make them what they aren't. But of course that's ridiculous. You can't change your metabolism or your bone structure. You can't change the color of your skin. Isn't that obvious? You would think so, but the people who don't look the right way have been deceived for so long they've lost the self-esteem that would protect them against the campaign that tells them they don't fit in. Putting people down is the American way. It's the capitalist system. An obsessive consumer is a dissatisfied person, a person who has been swindled out of the moral sense of who and what she is and believes she must be someone else. This is not clear thinking. It has to stop. Somebody somewhere needs to stand up and say, 'I am not thin but I am beautiful.' A child of an adult who is not thin should say"— Here Stella could feel her voice sticking in her throat—"I love you just the way you are. Thank you." She walked back to her seat and sat down. They started to clap.

After the speech they were supposed to do a critique. The speaker was to stay quiet until the end when he or she could respond to the comments. Mrs. Cleveland walked up to the front of the room and said, "That was a very dramatic, well-put-together speech, Stella, thank you."

"She looked out the window too much," one kid said. Someone else said, "It wasn't really controversial. I mean, I think it's pretty obvious."

Mrs. Cleveland said that was a good comment, but she wondered if everyone agreed with it. Was there anyone in the room who thought the topic was controversial? Martha answered that one. Maybe someone in her family was fat, too. "Kids are supposed to be the most important part of a family. But if one of the parents is obsessed with their weight they're not putting all of their attention where it should be going— on their kids."

Mrs. Cleveland told Martha that she was absolutely right. People who were overweight got the message from society that they couldn't be loved. And if they thought they couldn't be loved, how could they be good parents? "Who knows anything about the history of advertising in this country?" she asked. "How effective is it? Does it change people's lives? Ads teach us that drinking is okay, smoking is okay. This would be a good topic for a speech. Is there anyone here who hasn't picked a subject yet? All right, then everyone knows what they're going to talk about. Good. Stella, do you want to respond to any of the comments?"

Stella shook her head because she was still seeing her mother at the kitchen table, sitting in a cloud of cigarette smoke. She was a big pink lump, a blob, a mistake, a creature marooned on the island of her body. She was so fat that getting up from a chair and walking across the floor exhausted her.

Later, when Stella went into the cafeteria, she spotted Darryl sitting by himself at a table in the back. She sat down next to him and he slipped her a dollar bill under the table, which she stuck in her pocket. She left him to stand in the lunch line.

Before they met, she never ate in the cafeteria. She'd go into the bathroom and nibble on some celery with peanut butter or unwrap a napkin full of crackers and then spend the rest of the period in the library. One year she had filled out the form for free lunches and forged her mother's signature, but her mother had found out about it when a social worker called their home. The salary she had put down was ridiculously low and someone in the county decided to investigate. Even with the correct income figure they were still eligible. But her mother said no, thank you, she didn't want her daughter eating all of that greasy high-cholesterol cafeteria food. Stella might be thin now but she had the fat gene too, so from day one she had to be careful.

"Hey, girl," Darryl whispered when she returned with a tray of things her mother would not have approved of.

"Hey, yourself." She wanted to touch the sprinkling of freckles on his neck where his collar rubbed against them. Or the gully in his wrist where the veins were prominent. Those were the places on his body where she went for comfort. But she didn't this time. She still saw her mother in that smoky room.

Fourteen

In the faculty lounge Faith was telling Mel and Sarah about Stella's speech. "It just broke my heart. That poor girl. I thought she was going to cry. But she kept going and it was a good speech and there're probably a couple of kids in that class who appreciated it. Say, what about doing a unit on the role of advertising next year? Bring in its uses in the different mediums, its coercive powers. I think these kids are ready for it, I really do."

"Faithy, Faithy," Mel intoned. "We were going to do waste dumps and the environmental impact, remember? We were going to research the controversy around that dump in the old salt mine and go out there and interview the owners."

"This is closer to their lives. I think it would be very instructive for a lot of them. We could focus on how advertisements encourage a certain image. There's a lot of stuff here that they're struggling with every day."

"Let them struggle. They're teenagers. They're supposed to struggle. Let's not interrupt their private lives. Next thing you'll want is a unit on premarital sex with free condoms for anyone who asks."

"That would be a great idea."

"She's serious, isn't she?" Mel asked the rest of the table.

"Faith is always serious." Shelly, who was at the coffee machine, came over to them and said, "That's why I like her so much. She's a big-hearted serious woman and we need more of them around here, Mel."

"I just think we can't be scared of subjects like these. In a lot of these homes there aren't any clear-thinking adults. They're boozed-out or frantic about something like dieting."

"Oh God!" Mel covered his eyes. "What I had the misfortune of stumbling across on Main Street last week right in front of Better Days!"

"Stumbling, Mel?" Shelly said. "Why were you stumbling?"

"It's a figure of speech, sweetheart. I saw Mrs. Doyle in her bathrobe trying to get that old Cadillac started. Harry came out and saved her."

"Thank God for Harry," Faith said.

"What do you mean, thank God for Harry? He's not doing such a great service to this community. Happy hour every Friday? Two for the price of one every Saturday night?"

"Well, that's right," Faith conceded. "But he did get the car going, didn't he?"

"I gave him a lift to the service station and he bought her a gallon of gas."

Fifteen

~⌐

Harry was in the bar. The door was open, the jukebox was on, and peering in, she could see him in the back talking on the phone. He waved her inside. He said, "Jack, listen, let me call you back in an hour." Jack must have said something in return because Harry replied, "Priorities. My priorities are always in the right place." He lowered his voice to say something about her, she was sure, and then he hung up the phone. "Beautiful lady!"

"You're forgetting, Harry. I'm not beautiful. I'm very plain-looking."

"Hey, sexy hunk of woman, get over here!"

"May I close the door first?"

"I was just trying to get some of that nice October sunshine to come in. But go ahead, propriety first, close the door."

"You have a story to tell me?" She walked across the room,

past the booths and pool tables to the old-fashioned wooden bar that ran across the back wall.

"Sure do!"

She took her coat off and sat on a stool.

"Nothing much, of course, but I did close that window."

"You got up there?" When he nodded, she said, "Oh, I'm so excited, tell me everything. How did you get in?"

"I opened the door on the alley, walked up the stairs, opened the door at the top of the stairs, walked across the floor, closed the window, walked back across the floor, opened the door, closed it behind me, and walked back down the stairs." Suddenly he saw her sitting on top of the bar with her skirt off and her bare legs raised on his shoulders. A man was due to check the beer cooler in half an hour but that didn't matter. Such a thing as he was thinking of could be done in half an hour. He could simply lock the front door. Of course, she wouldn't want to because she was on her lunch break. She'd be afraid of carrying a smell back to work with her. A smell-conscious woman, obsessed with it. Silly because sex wears off so quickly.

"Well, what was up there? Tell me what you saw."

"Cardboard boxes. Clothes racks. Hangers. I saw their footprints in the dust."

"You did?"

He knew she was about to ask to see them herself, so he quickly added, "I scuffed them out when I walked on top of them. Sorry, Helene. I was kind of rushed, I wanted to get out of there."

"Was it creepy?"

"Just a dusty, forgotten place."

"So tell me about it."

"I'm not a very good storyteller. Why don't you tell me the story? And while you tell me the story…"

She leaned in closer. "While I tell you the story…"

He opened the top button of her blouse. "I want to look at you."

"I have to be at work in an hour."

"And I have a refrigeration man coming, but I want to look at you. Here, just slip out of your blouse."

She knew then that she would arrive at the post office with her cheeks bright, her neck flushed, and a musty scent deep down underneath her clothes. She would worry about it until the crush of customers washed it out of her mind.

In the afternoon, after waiting on people in the front, it was her turn to sort the mail. Moving from the table to the cubbyholes, she felt the glow that he had kindled finally settle back into her skin and she could follow an idea to a straight and sober conclusion. Mail she could do in any condition; it was her preoccupations that floated away from her until the flush of lovemaking settled. Finally relaxed, finally slowed down, she let her mind fill with random pictures: She saw the maple tree behind William's house with the piece of rope she hung the chickens on swinging in the breeze, then the orange lamplight at the back of the bar and all of the bottles reflected in the mirror behind the cash register. She saw the girl in the red dress standing at the window, her hand at her neck and the boy walking up behind her and the words Baldwin Mercantile above their heads. She pictured William walking down the street next to Buster, rocking side to side like a duck waddling. She pictured her mother standing outside the house on a warm spring afternoon, with the green apron on and a piece of cloth holding back her hair. Her rubber boots were covered with mud because she'd been planting peas in the garden. What swam into her vision next she almost tried to stop. She would have stopped it if she hadn't been with Harry that morning. Now she was too loose. So the next thing that came into her mind were the dark spires on a church in Hamburg. The facade had survived the bombing, but the rest of the church was a temporary wooden structure. She was passing through the enormous wooden door to the interior. She walked down the aisle, knelt in front of the altar, crossed herself, and sat down on one of the pews. Only to think. She was eight years old and her mother and brother must have been close by. But it felt as though she was entirely alone.

Two important things had just come into her life then and she needed to go over them by herself. The first was a letter her mother had received from a cousin in America and the second was the understanding that she must have had a father. Was it the same father the baby Gunter had? Her mother had never said. Helene knew why. Her father was a spirit and spirit fathers didn't like to be called by one name because they lived in so many places at once. Her spirit father was sorry he couldn't be with her because he loved her, but he sent substitutes and told her to watch out for them. One was the enormous chestnut tree in front of the church; it too had survived the bombing. She liked to stand under its branches and watch the cars. She knew it was one of her substitute fathers because it made her feel safe and welcome. She decided she would bring the tree a present. She would give it her favorite butter cookies, which she would wrap in a piece of cloth and bind with another piece of cloth tied into a bow. She would lay the present down at the foot of the tree. That's what she did the next day. But she put it in the crook of the lowest branch because she was afraid that if she put it on the ground a dog would steal it.

The next thing she saw was their cabin on the ship that they took to America. It smelled like bacon and potatoes because it was down on the lowest level, next to the kitchen where her mother worked to pay for their passage. She never got sick on the boat; in fact, during the first day of their voyage, while Gunter and her mother lay on their bunks ill, she was the one to bring them water. But the motion sickness came to her finally on the bus to this town, to Paris. She stood over the tiny sink and heaved up all the contents of her stomach until only clear bile ran down the drain. Her cheeks stayed hot the entire trip and she slept with her head on her mother's lap. When the bus pulled into town, nobody was there to meet them. Nobody was home at the phone number their mother had carried in her purse for so many months. They huddled together under the gray American sky and waited two hours for their German cousin to pick them up.

Finally, they had gone into the hardware store. The man there shook his head when Uta asked him if there were any hotels in Paris. "Nope, you'd have to go the ten miles to Sharon and the bus for Sharon only comes once a day and it's already left."

"Taxi?" Uta asked in careful English. "You have taxi?"

"Taxi service? No ma'am, not in Paris, New York. It's too

small for taxi service. Got to go to your big cities like Los Angeles, California, if you want taxi service." He chuckled with a man standing at the counter who looked so strange Helene had been afraid to glance at him. He wore pants that came up around his shoulders.

Uta ushered them out of the store. They'd left their suit-cases on the sidewalk in front along with the big striped bag containing the remains of the food they'd packed for the bus. They stood by it now, Uta saying again that she had written Cousin Dagmar the two possible days of their arrival and maybe he had decided to drive over and pick them up but the car had run out of gas. Maybe he lived far away from Paris. His address hadn't been Paris, though he had told her to take the bus to Paris. But maybe his car had stopped working and he was as stranded as they were with no way of getting in touch. Such a thing was possible.

Fear was not unusual. Helene felt it so often she could almost pretend it wasn't there. But Gunter just stood on the sidewalk and cried. Uta gave them each one of the small suit-cases to carry, picked up the large one as well as the striped bag, and started off at a brisk walk. They walked more slowly behind her. Cars on the street slowed down to look at them and though she and Gunter turned around and stared back, Uta marched ahead. That, Helene realized, had been her moth-er's greatest attribute: the ability to step out into uncertainty and trust that she would survive. They walked past the grocery store, the drugstore, the gas station, the ladies' wear shop, and at the other end of the street, just before the residential neighborhood, Uta had finally slowed down in front of the bookstore. She liked books. When she opened the door for the children, maybe she had been just tired and desperate enough to think that among the books lining the shelves, there would be some in German. But they forgot about books when they noticed William.

In Hamburg their neighbor in the shack across from them had been a dwarf. To find another Mr. Pfeiffer all the way across the ocean in New York State had to be a piece of luck. The warmth of the store after the cold afternoon felt good to them. William walked out from behind the desk and told them to set their suitcases down next to the door. "You look like you've come a long way."

"Deutschland," Uta said.

"That *is* a long way. My goodness, sit down."

"Ve drive on the bus to meet the relative."

"To meet your relative? Maybe I know him. What's his name?"

"Excuse please. Please to speak slow."

"What's...his...name...your relative?"

"Dagmar Rosenbauer."

"Well, it doesn't sound familiar. Where does he live?"

Uta opened her enormous pocketbook and fished around in the bottom until she brought up the crumpled piece of paper that Helene knew was the letter she'd received almost six months ago. "Here," she said, handing it over to William so he could look at the address on the envelope.

"Well, that's only down the road a piece. Does he know you're here?"

"Ve have telephone but no man to answer."

"Tell you what. In half an hour I'm going to close up and it just so happens I'm heading out in that same direction."

"No good. I have telephone much. No man to home."

"That's not surprising," William said. "In these parts, you can't trust the telephone."

Uta looked confused.

"Some of the time it doesn't work. Or else you're not there. You're out at the barn and can't hear it. I'm sure he's home. He wouldn't leave if he knew you were coming. He must be home."

"Yes, this day or the next day the bus. I said in the letter."

"See, he just went out to the barn. He wouldn't go away. He would stay home the two days. Probably his phone doesn't work."

"Please?"

"His phone. It's broken."

Uta was so relieved to hear that she blushed. She called Gunter and Helene over and told them not to worry, that soon everything was going to be all right and they should be quiet (which they were already) and look at books.

The farmhouse William took them to was at the end of a deeply rutted road that looked like it hadn't been driven over in a long time. The yard was overgrown. The unpainted house with two blank windows on either side of a thin wooden door looked run-down and empty. Nevertheless, they got out and walked up to the porch, Uta calling out in German. The front door opened when she pulled at it and the children followed her into the cold house. It was empty. An old couch, a wooden chair with a pair of men's suspenders draped over it, and in the kitchen, a book lying on the table—there was nothing more. Uta picked up the book eagerly, but it was in English.

An examination of the rooms upstairs revealed only that the last occupant had been a man; there were razor blades resting on the basin in the bathroom and one large wool sock pushed into a dusty corner. The children trailed after Uta back down the stairs. Helene could see that the situation was serious so she stayed quiet, but Gunter cried, he was hungry and tired of traveling. Uta picked him up and joggled him up and down in her arms. She took his feet out of his tiny boots and kissed them. Then she brushed back his hair, saying in German, "You poor little boy, you poor little boy," over and over. Helene saw a broom in the corner of the room and started to knock the cobwebs off the walls.

Sixteen

~~~

What William saw when he finally got tired of sitting in his truck outside the abandoned farmhouse was an industriousness he associated with secure, happy feelings. Despite the cold and filth of the room, the little girl was sweeping down cobwebs. The mother was walking back and forth across the room, jiggling the little boy, who was sobbing steadily, up and down. William noticed again how short she was. She was a hefty little woman and she seemed strong and determined. Maybe she was determined enough to decide to live there. But they wouldn't last through the winter without meat or wood. Whereas he had meat and wood and a house big enough for all four of them. He pulled up a crate, gestured to her to sit down, and extended his hand. "We never introduced ourselves before. My name is William Swick."

She shook hands with him and said, "Uta Hugel. Helene."

Helene curtsied. "Gunter Hugel." Gunter stopped crying long enough to look at him.

"I don't know quite how to say this," William began, "but it seems to me that this cousin of yours has disappeared and it would be foolish, to my way of thinking, to set yourself up here to wait for him."

"Please to speak slow," Uta said. "My English very young."

William cleared his throat. "You can't stay here. You need wood and there isn't wood. You need food and there isn't food." As she looked at him, her blue eyes bright from the cold, he found himself staring. They seemed brighter next to the angry red of her wind-chapped cheeks. "My house is very big. Please come to my house."

Expecting her to resist, he was prepared with reasons, but she simply said very carefully, "Thank you." Helene put the broom back in the corner, Gunter stopped crying and allowed her to put his boots back on his feet and set him down, and Uta stood up and pulled her scarves tighter around her throat.

They said nothing on the drive back to the main road and continued in silence as he turned up his road and drove up the driveway. They came in through the wood room and stopped at the threshold of his large clean kitchen. Uta looked around. Then she said, "The children, to sleep, please." He led her up a steep flight of stairs to the two small unused rooms on the second floor. There was a bed in only one of them, but it would be fine for the whole family the first night. If they were going to stay, he would see about finding another bed.

Seventeen

~~~

*T*hree months after the bombing, when the Russians occupied Dresden, Uta had worked along with the other
women clearing away the rubble. There were seventeen million
cubic meters of it, a city in itself, and for many months she
shoveled it into her wheelbarrow and dumped it into the
waiting trucks. Where did they take it? She never asked.
Maybe they loaded it onto a barge and sailed it down the Elbe
River to the North Sea. And maybe the entire city, in all of its
millions of pieces, was down on the sandy floor of that great
body of cold water. After working in the wreckage, she'd pick
Helene up at the waiting place for the children of the women
who shoveled, and they'd go stand in food lines and then go
back to the basement where they lived under one big piece of
cardboard and two old wooden doors. That was the only roof
they had. Water seeped in everywhere.

Uta wept continuously. She wept for such a long time that

she began to wonder if it would ever stop. Would she ever feel something else?

Neighborhood by neighborhood, the rubble was cleared away and all evidence of the baroque architecture the city was famous for was gone. With nothing beautiful anywhere to look at—the city of small winding streets and hidden gardens was a wide-open expanse now with a wall still standing here and there and a few remaining shells of buildings—she realized that her sadness was the only way she had to keep what had been lost close to her. It was a way of not accepting the Russian authorities, not accepting the basement where the rain dripped down around them, not accepting the long tedious hours she spent at her next job, which was working in the hospital delivering food and medicine, not accepting the government nursery school where Helene spent her days while Uta worked.

One afternoon when she was at a store, she saw a stack of notebooks with lined pages and thin black covers. They were the same notebooks she had used for school when she was a child, the same notebooks all German children used. And now, after all that had happened, there they were again. She bought one and that night, when Helene was asleep on the cot, she sat at her makeshift table under the glimmer of the kerosene lamp and opened the notebook. As she picked up a pen and looked at the blank page a calm washed over her. She sat up very straight but the calmness didn't go away; it spread through her chest, relaxing her. What appeared in her mind, very distinctly, was a photograph that used to hang on the wall behind her bed. It was a formal portrait of her mother standing under an arbor. She looked mischievous, her smile suggesting there were secrets she and nobody else was privy to. Uta tried to create it in words so that she could always have it with her. Then she described the music her neighbor, Frau Singer, would play sometimes all afternoon long. Every Sunday her apartment was filled with Frau Singer's music. If it was summer it came in through the windows from the apartment downstairs and if it was winter, it issued up through the heat vents. They were folk songs and dance pieces and the light happy tunes would weave in and out, sometimes soft, sometimes loud.

The third thing she described in the notebook was an apartment building collapsing in front of her eyes and a sofa covered in flames shooting out from one of the windows. Glass was falling everywhere and when she looked again she saw the sofa hanging in a tree.

She fit all of those things on the first page because Uta's writing was small and cramped. On the second page she described the picture she sometimes saw in her dreams. It was a hand and part of an arm resting in a field full of buttercups and bedstraw. As soon as she saw the hand she knew it had belonged to Helene's father, who had been shot down in a plane over England. Although he had had large fleshy hands and hairy arms, the hand in the field was slender and feminine looking. Yet she knew it belonged to him. It was what his hand had become. It was the essence of him. There was a butterfly perched on the tip of his first finger, opening and closing its wings, but every time she sat down to talk to it—because the butterfly, too, was connected to Helene's father—it flew away.

The second thing she described on the second page was the iron gate along the Grosser Garten, the flowers and shrubbery pressing against it on one side and on the other, along the sidewalk, the canopy of leaves over her head from the chestnut trees. The sidewalk there was green and mossy, the air was cool, and she would often stand still at that spot, listening to the splash of water in the fountain.

She wrote about all of those memories that first night and when she looked at the notebook in the morning, not to read it but simply to see that it existed, she had a feeling almost like happiness. That was a start. If she could have a feeling like happiness, maybe one day happiness would come.

Uta didn't think she could go back to the spot where she used to live. She had avoided it for six months and soon they would be clearing the rubble away in that part of the city. The husband of the family that shared the basement with her told her that one wall of the hospital was still standing and if her building had been across from the hospital, she might be able to locate the exact spot where it stood.

She didn't even bring a shovel. She thought she would just look on the top of things. If there was nothing she could identify, so be it. And there wasn't. It was a heap of blackened wood and stone and glass. There wasn't a fragment of anything that had belonged to her. She saw other people's things, but nothing that had been hers. So she put that in the notebook, too. Of all that had been, there was nothing left, not a book, not a picture frame. Everything she once had, she carried inside her now. There was nothing external anymore. Strangely enough, after she visited the rubble that had once been the place where she lived, the purpose of the notebook became clear to her. As she began to fill the pages, which she did more rapidly now because all she had to do was name something and then she would remember, she felt herself growing emptier and emptier and as she began to empty out, she started to feel a purpose.

Although she called it *Verlorene Sachen, Lost Things*, the irony was that they weren't lost at all. They still existed because she had given them a place. And as she put down all that had once been, she realized that as soon as she finished, as soon as she had transferred everything from her memory to the page, she would be free to imagine a different kind of life for herself.

When she had the dream again and saw the hand in the field she understood finally that it didn't belong to Helene's father after all. It was her hand and the butterfly was beckoning her to follow it.

And then, suddenly, when Helene was seven years old and the war had been over for two years, she was pregnant again. It was the consequence of a single night when she had been desperately lonely. She hadn't thought such difficult living conditions and meager food would allow conception to happen. But it had. The father, a soldier, was soon shipped out and when he left, there was nothing any longer to keep her in the city where she no longer had a home or relatives or close friends. She and Helene went to Hamburg. It was in the English zone and she had heard there was better housing there and more food. Also, if the rubble of Dresden had been put on barges and taken down the Elbe River to the North Sea, Hamburg would have been the last city it passed. It was the doorway out of Germany. Maybe for the rubble and maybe for her.

So, when she was settled in Hamburg, she wrote a letter to a cousin in America. All she could remember of his address was Paris, New York, and she remembered that because it had seemed so wrong. But as wrong as it might have been, the letter got there, because three months later she received a reply. By that time, Gunter was born. During his infancy, when they lived in a small wooden shack that stayed dry during rainstorms, she filled another eight notebooks, which made thirteen altogether.

In the fourteenth, she was writing about a time from many years ago at the Brülsche Terrasse where she had gone with her mother to have tea on a summer evening and watch the boats go past and listen to the quartet that played in front of the Albertinum. It was 1940, just after Hitler had invaded France. Her mother's face was in the shadows. She was holding Uta's hand and she was saying, "Isn't this a splendid moment? Look at the children swimming!" Uta looked at the children wading in from the grassy shore to a shallow bathing spot. She smoothed out her dress, which was stained with blueberry juice because they had been in the garden that afternoon picking blueberries, and told her mother, "I am going to have a baby."

There wasn't anything else to put in the book after that. She didn't need to describe her mother's shocked expression or her discussions with Helene's father, Wolff, about marriage. She had decided to remain by herself and raise the baby with her mother's help. It was a decision she came to gradually and she didn't need to write about that either. Those were things that could have happened anywhere. What she needed was the visuals—her mother's face, the trees along the Elbe River, the sight of the quartet in front of the museum, the memory of Wolff's wonderful thick body. The soldiers, the raids, the food lines, Hitler's voice on the radio—none of those things made it into the notebook. It was the images of her own past that she needed to secure. And that day, when she described the Terrasse and remembered how her mother held her hand as they watched the children swimming, she was finished. Soon after that, she wrote to her cousin and asked if he would sponsor her to come to Paris in America. Three months later, a letter came back with the answer yes. He told her he was renting a house that had two floors that were all his and there was land outside to put in a garden. He was doing seasonal farmwork so he traveled a lot but there was plenty of room for her, too, and he would help her find a job. She wrote back and told him that she had almost enough money saved. One day, standing in a line for butter, she heard about a coal ship that sailed to America twice a month and hired women to do kitchen work. She went to the shipping office to apply for a job and then she gave up some of the money she was saving to buy a book to learn English.

In the last letter she received from Dagmar, he told her that she should take a bus from New York City to Paris and he gave her his phone number and explained where the bus came in and where she could find a telephone. The next time she wrote him was five months later when she had a date for their departure and was packing up their belongings. She gave him two possible days for her arrival. With the letter posted, she faced the task of stuffing their essential possessions into bags they would be able to carry. It would not be possible to take the fourteen notebooks. Should she mail them? She discovered it would be too expensive. So she decided to pack only the first notebook. The rest she would dispose of.

That night the hand with the butterfly appeared again in

her dream. So the day before she was to leave forever, she carried the thirteen notebooks in a paper bag, and took a bus out past neighborhood after neighborhood of squat gray apartment buildings where electric wires covered the sky and children played in weedy lots and there weren't any flowers or shrubs or trees. At the last stop she got out. She passed a dark-shuttered store that sold groceries and she went in to buy a bottle of soda because she was thirsty. Then she walked out past the last apartment building into a field where wildflowers were growing, mint and vervain. She took the notebooks out of the bag and placed each one on the ground.

Eighteen

*E*very time Stella entered the drugstore she felt better. The possibilities gave her hope. She stood in the cosmetics aisle, surveying lipstick and eye shadow, then she moved to the hair-supplies aisle and looked at hair bands and barrettes and shampoos. She never thought about what she wanted; it was never that clear. She just looked at each item and waited to see if a picture of Darryl formed in her mind and if it did, she slipped whatever she had been looking at into her coat pocket. She always made herself buy something afterwards: a pretzel or a piece of gum. That was all she could afford because the only money she ever had was the pocket change she picked up from the floor of her mother's car or took out of the pockets of her mother's supermarket uniform when she was doing the laundry. The drugstore also sold a few necklaces and earrings, all of which she'd stolen already. Every time she went back she hoped that maybe they had gotten in more.

She kept a tab on her petty crimes and in the six months she'd been stealing she'd only taken thirty-six dollars' worth of goods. As soon as she had thirty-six dollars she would pay Mr. Taflin back. Of course, that would have to be the day she moved out of town because once you confessed to being a kleptomaniac you couldn't continue to live in the same place. Mr. Taflin would never trust her to be in his drugstore again.

It was the day after she'd made her speech in the class and it was cold and bleak. She'd stepped into the drugstore mostly for warmth. She was tired of her usual aisles, so she stood by the newspapers and then inched her way down to magazines. Above the magazines, there were a few games: checkers, Parcheesi, cards, Scrabble. She pictured Darryl bent over a Scrabble board. They were playing together, she who had never played Scrabble in her life and was certain she wouldn't be intelligent enough to manage it, and he who could invent solutions out of thin air. It was the kind of game other people's parents played with their children to make them word-smart. She glanced up to check each end of the aisle, and slipped the box into her book bag. With the top of it sticking out in plain view, she bought two pretzels, flashing old Mr. Taflin a smile as she said, "No thanks, I don't need a bag."

The sidewalk was empty and the day was still cold and dismal. Now what she needed was a dictionary because to play a game like Scrabble you needed help. Darryl's family had lots of dictionaries but she couldn't ask him to lend her one. She'd have to check one out of the library. She saw the time on the bank clock; it would probably still be open, so she walked in the other direction toward the ostentatious pillared building that held the Paris public library. The ceiling in the main room was very high and up on what used to be the stage of the opera house it had originally been, there were now chairs and tables and along the walls, shelves of reference books. She found a one-volume Webster's, sat down at one of the tables, and took out her Scrabble board. Then she studied the directions. She dealt seven tiles for herself and seven tiles for her partner. Her partner went first and out of his seven she spelled *cup*. From *cup* she made *up*. Already she could tell that she was going to be embarrassingly stupid. She made a plural out of *cup* by adding an *s*. She decided to scratch that game and start a new one. With the dictionary's help, her opponent's first word was *exile*. From that she made *oxen*. She thought of that one by herself. From *oxen* she made *love*. That was her own, too. Then she made *languid*.

The moon was hanging outside the windows, watching her. She felt liquid, which was a word she would have liked to use, but she couldn't, so she did *hair* instead, feeling even more liquid as she sat wrapped in her chair, her long legs, long hair, and everything else that she was, focused on the moon as she put one smart word after another on her board. At ten to nine the librarian flickered the lights. Stella packed her stuff back up and put on her jacket. Outside on the steps she wondered what she might do that night for dinner. Even if she had money, the restaurant was closed. So she walked under the velvet sky towards nowhere and at the intersection where she could either proceed straight to her house or make a turn to go to Darryl's, she chose the turn. He wasn't supposed to see friends on school nights. He was supposed to do homework. But she would like to explain to his mother that they weren't friends, they were lovers. She walked down the block, past windows that were curtained against the darkness. A cat yowled in someone's backyard. A dog barked, and in a bay window she saw a family gathered around a blue television screen, the parents on the couch and the kids sitting on the rug with the dog. They looked warm and well fed. At Darryl's house, light fell over the sidewalk and the branches of the maple tree in the front yard cast shadows across the grass. She walked across them and crept around to the back, dry leaves crunching under her footsteps. It didn't matter. Their dog was so old she was deaf. At the back of the house, behind the terrace, there was a beech tree twice the size of the maple in the front. Its branches started low to the ground and were spaced upwards along the thick gnarled trunk like stairs. It was the tree Darryl's mother had saved from the chain saws when they were building the addition. She'd insisted the design be altered so the builder wouldn't have to cut through its roots to excavate for the basement. According to Darryl, his mother told the whole story to her dinner parties and then invited the guests, at whatever time of year it was, out to the back terrace to admire the tree.

"I spared no expense for this tree," his mother would tell her shivering friends. "It cost us twenty thousand dollars to save it. The basement was supposed to come out to here, which clearly, even this far away, would have compromised the root system. So the basement is only under the back bedroom, and the den and laundry room are on a concrete slab. Pouring a slab required no digging at all. So I think the tree was happy. Weren't you?" she'd ask, looking up at the beech admiringly.

Besides being huge, it also made an excellent ladder to Darryl's second-floor window over the garage. Stella dropped her book bag at the bottom and swung herself up to the first branch. From there she hoisted herself up to the second, slid down to the crotch and stepped over to the next branch. Then she pulled herself up to the one above that. The only tricky moment was at the top when she had to creep down the length of one of the limbs to get close enough to tap on the window. She hoped the lamplight spilling out into the night meant that he was inside, working. The branch was thinner out at that end but as long as she didn't look down, she knew she was okay. She'd done this once before and she trusted herself. The moon was her accomplice. She gripped the branch between her legs and moved herself along it, pushing with her hands. Her pants were catching on all the nubs and twigs, but there wasn't anything she could do about it now. As smooth as it was, the bark was burning her thighs even through the material. She loosened her legs and pulled herself forward. For a second, she swung to the side, but she caught herself just in time and straightened up. She could see into his room now. He wasn't at his desk. Had she risked her life for nothing? Maybe he was on his bed. She couldn't tell from the outside, but she was close enough to the window to tap it, so clinging with her legs, she took her left hand off the limb and knocked lightly on the glass. A shadow moved. Maybe it was his father. But no, it was her adored one, his hair tousled because he'd been lying down. He pulled the sash up and lifted her over the windowsill. They fell onto each other's mouths. When they pulled apart she said, "I haven't had any dinner and I just climbed that enormous tree."

An hour later, when the rest of the house had retired for the night, she was eating Darryl's mother's lasagna, which he had reheated for her in the oven, along with a heap of broccoli, a couple slices of French bread, and some fancy kind of cheese.

It was more food than she had eaten in one sitting in a while and the first time in ages that she'd had a vegetable, unless of course you counted overcooked peas from the cafeteria. She went slowly, one bite at a time. She was sitting on the floor with her back against his bed and her legs straight out in front of her. Darryl was lying down perpendicular to her with his head in her lap. "Tell your mother for me this is delicious. I've never had it homemade before. It's neat the way there's spinach and stuff in it." She leaned over and kissed him. Then she picked up his wrist to look at the time. "Eleven-thirty! Shit, mom gets off at twelve."

"Like she's really going to notice if you're not there."

He didn't understand the maybes. Maybe she would. There was one time that Stella could remember when she did. So maybe she would again. It wasn't all just one way or the other. There was an in-between place. Not to mention the other place where the things you wanted sometimes actually happened. "She might. Sometimes she comes up to see if I'm in bed."

"Sometimes she can't even remember you exist."

Even though it was true, she resented the picture he had of her family. "She's my mom. Are you going to take me down to the front door or not?"

"Just stay. You don't have to go. Just relax for once, will you?"

There was a painting by that artist he liked over his bed. She hoped Darryl wouldn't paint the way he did, with things not making sense, because then she wouldn't be able to understand him. She pointed to his wall and said, "I don't like that guy." The painting was of a man standing on a bridge. There were wings on his shoulders and a lion sitting behind him.

"Magritte? You should like him. He's painting your life, Stella. Why don't you just face it? Want to see this picture I did of you?"

"You painted me? Sure I want to see it."

He lifted up the flounce that hung around the bottom of his bed and pulled out a huge piece of paper. She saw her black hair, her dark skin, and her green eyes. Her mouth was open as though she was talking, but there were pink blossoms spilling out of it, some of them getting stuck in her teeth. "Why'd you make me look so weird?"

"Well..." He glanced up at her sheepishly. "Everyone knows what you look like in real life. So why should I paint the way you really look? I'm the only one, at least I think I'm the only one, who knows what it feels like to kiss you. Am I the only one?"

She slapped his hand. "Of course you're the only one. Don't be silly."

"I thought so. And I just—well, when it's happening, I think of these huge waxy brilliant buds that are going to open one day as soon as the sun lets them."

"That's really nice, Darryl." She touched his leg. "But couldn't you have painted them behind me or something? How come they have to be coming out of my mouth like that?"

"Because it happens when we're Frenching. I smell them when I get close to your face." He slipped his arm around her. "Hey, you should be flattered. What other girl has these beautiful pansy buds living under her tongue?"

So maybe it was true. Maybe there was a place down inside her where there were black carefully weeded beds of earth and row after row of brilliant flowers growing in them. Somebody came along every day and watered them and staked them up so that they would be tall and uncluttered and healthy. It was someone with a kind disposition and enormous patience and very nimble fingers. Certainly not herself. Not her mother either. In her mind, she placed a word going across: *gardener* and another one moving down and sharing the d: *guardian*. How happy she felt. She could give in and be those flowers and spend the whole night with her leaves wrapped around him. Before daylight, she would sneak out and walk home. But what if by some miracle her mother decided to check on her? "Two conditions, then maybe I'll stay."

"What are they?"

"One, you walk me down to the front door when it's time to go and two, we play Scrabble. With a dictionary, okay, because that way it's educational."

"That's crazy. It takes too long with a dictionary. And since when does the girl of the flowers play Scrabble?"

"Since a long time. It's one of my favorite games."

"You told me you didn't like it."

"I didn't. But I do now."

"Why don't we play strip Scrabble? If your word has three letters or less you have to take off a piece of your clothes."

"Let me go put on my sweater."

He grabbed her leg. "No way, no padding. Just how you are."

Nineteen

~~~

The Germans had slept on the bed in the upstairs bedroom two nights in a row. He taught them English in the evenings and it seemed as though the girl could pick it up quickly. Uta had washed his kitchen floor and cooked dinner and despite himself, William started to think about how pleasant life might be if they stayed. But she clearly wasn't planning on settling in. Yesterday, she had called the number she kept in her pocketbook six times. That morning she had tried it three times and them in the evening she sat down at the table in the kitchen and tried it again. No one answered.

William could sense her desperation. He picked up the slip of paper with the phone number and said, "Let me try it." He dialed the operator and asked her to check the number. It was just as he thought. He said, "Thank you very much" and hung up. "The number has been disconnected. Nobody lives at this number anymore. All right? Now let me try something else."

He dialed information. But there wasn't anyone named Dagmar Rosenbauer in their area. "Your cousin doesn't have a telephone here, I'm sorry."

"I have to find him."

"Well, that's going to take time so settle in here for now. We'll find another bed and we'll get the kids registered at school. If you want, we can put a notice in the paper asking for the whereabouts of this Dagmar, but my guess is that he's far away."

"Please," Uta said. "I understand little little."

"You stay here," William repeated. He spread his arms out. "Big house. Lots of room."

"I cannot. No money. Children, I. No family."

"That's okay. I don't mind it and actually I'd enjoy the company. The house is too big for just one person."

"Okay, for you I vork. I cook. I clean. I vash. I make nicen, yes?"

William touched her on the shoulder and said the first thing that came into his head: "Bless you." He who believed in nature rather than God. Maybe he had known, back then, how she was going to change his life.

Twenty

~

A s the days and weeks went on and they continued to live in William's house it never occurred to Helene that this short kind man might be one of her substitute fathers. Though he felt as safe and welcoming as the chestnut tree in Hamburg, she could tell that it was her mother that his attention was focused on, not her.

One night, after they had been there almost six months, when she was already an American schoolgirl and could almost speak English, she lay in the narrow iron bed she shared with Uta, waiting for the comfortable rustle of her mother's clothes as she prepared for bed. But the floor never creaked under her mother's footsteps and Helene eventually was too tired to listen anymore and fell asleep. What she might have heard if the door at the bottom of the stairs had been open was a man's scream. And if she had been too scared to fall asleep after that, she would have heard the weeping.

Twenty-One

*U*ta was driving, and because she was a nervous driver, she was going very slowly and carefully down Eastern Road. There were six points of danger and she never felt relaxed until she'd passed them all. When the danger was upon her, she exerted extra caution, slowing down even more and being especially vigilant as she glanced about. The first danger was a sharp turn, the second was a slight downhill before another turn where she always put her foot on the brake, the third was two gentle curves, one after the other, the fourth was a hidden driveway, and the fifth was a spot where the valley spread out in the distance and met the hill. It was such a beautiful vista she had to remind herself to keep her eyes on the road. The sixth was the tiny rise she was just then approaching where her view of any cars coming from the opposite direction was blocked.

What she was thinking about in the last moments she was going to be alive was the night she had invited William to sit with her. The children were in bed and she had made a pot of raspberry tea and set out two pieces of the lemon cake she'd baked the day before. He sat down at the table and looked at her as intently as he had when they were in the abandoned farmhouse. That first time, she had been afraid he was going to leave them there but if that was what he had decided, she knew she'd be able to bear it. To go with him if he invited them or to stay there if he didn't—either way, it wouldn't have been easy. So she looked back at him, not turning away until he did first. In Dresden, after the war, when the fabric of life had come unraveled, looking like that at a man was to invite his attention. That might have been what she was doing in the farmhouse and maybe it had worked. It got them where they were now.

The second time, she interrupted her looking with a word. Helene had been teaching her more English words. "Tea, please," she said, handing him the cup. "Cake." She didn't take hers, though; she sat still and watched him from under her bangs. She'd been watching him steadily for six months, trying to figure out what the body looked like that lived in the clothes she washed once a week along with their own. She'd decided it was no different from any others she'd seen. It had all the right parts; it just lacked the familiar distance between them. What she needed now was to tell him something very important, but she didn't know the English. When they first moved there, she would say something to him in German, hoping that it would sound enough like English that he would understand, but it never worked. So when she didn't have the English, she showed him with her hands what she wanted to say. Now, she put her hand on her heart and whispered in German all the things she had been storing up. *That she had noticed...that she felt...that* *she wanted...*It all came out in a rush of language that he didn't understand. She didn't know the simple word *love*. Helene had never taught it to her and she had been afraid to ask. So she described it as best she could in paragraphs of German. He looked at her blankly. In frustration, she pulled out the piece of cloth tying her hair back. Next she took off the leather vest she always wore to protect her against the drafts. Then she took off her slippers and stood up to pull down her woolen stockings. She unpinned her skirt and stepped out of it. He sat across from her, watching, but there was an expression on his face she didn't understand. Fear? Could it be that he was afraid? She was in her blouse and her underpants and she was feeling so much for him, and she wanted him to touch her. He only reached the middle of her torso so she kneeled down next to him. He put his hand on the top of her head. But she turned her head up, moved his hand to her neck, and kissed him. After she kissed him, she took off her blouse and her undergarments. She stood in front of him naked, but he did nothing. So, hoping she wasn't too big or too heavy, she sat down on his lap, her bosom in his face.

Still, he didn't seem to know what to do with her. Maybe he didn't like the way she looked. But it was the body other men had enjoyed. It hadn't changed. It was the body her children had been conceived in and which the two fathers, one of them definitely dead and the location of the other just as uncertain, had made love to many times. She had not changed. She was as round and full as before and even after two babies her skin wasn't any less tight or smooth. She wanted him to show her that he was pleased but he showed her nothing. No sign of what he felt was on his face. She got off his lap and stood up. He stood up, too. She bent down to retrieve her clothing but her vest slipped out of the bundle. As she bent down again to pick it up, she felt his hand on her buttocks. It slipped between her legs and around to her front. He was touching her, pressing her, massaging. She went down on her hands and knees, and guided his fingers to the right place. He didn't know what to do so she showed him. She could feel him fumbling with his own clothing. Then he mounted her from behind and began thrusting.

She had happiness over and over, but he seemed unable to release himself. The floor was hard under her knees; she was tired of being in that position. It was much later, when the moon outside the window had reached the top of the sky and sent a ray of blue light into the kitchen, that he screamed. That was how she knew he was done. She was afraid he had woken the children. But when he stopped, the house was quiet. Except for his sobbing, which grew louder and more embarrassing as it went on. He was like the man she'd been with after the war who was Gunter's father. But then they both had wept. They had wept together. The pleasure had recalled all of their pain. She didn't weep now. Enough of the weeping. She couldn't imagine what it was that this American man who had never been in the war was crying about. Didn't he have everything he needed? She turned around and knelt beside him. She was giddy from sudden lightness, happy, carefree, except she had very sore knees. They hugged one another. He lifted her breasts, one at a time, weighing them in his hands, and then he kissed them.

Twenty-Two

*E*very night in his sleep William was ready to draw out his sword and conquer the world. He would beat back the gang of boys who had taunted him on the playground when he was a child. Except most of them had died in the war, so what was the use? Then there were the girls who had waited for him after school and walked behind him chanting, "Little boy blue, come blow your horn. Little boy blue, come blow your horn. Little boy blue, do you have a horn?" He was going to corner each one of them now and pull their long hair. Then he was going to mount them from the back and fuck them hard and leave them on the sidewalk.

What was the use? One of them had five kids before she had turned twenty-two and an alcoholic husband who gave her black eyes. Another died in a car crash when she was nineteen and the third moved away right after high school and never returned, not even for funerals.

He would smash his fist into the bellies of the people at the shopping center in Sharon who stared. Or maybe he would just stare back at them. Maybe he'd point them out to Helene and Gunter. Helene, at eleven, was taller than he was. "See, there's a tall man," he'd say, and sweeping a protective arm around Gunter, who was only three, he'd quickly usher them in the other direction.

He would strangle the nurse at the hospital who had shrieked when she came into the bathroom where he was doubled over with cramps. And just left him there. So he'd pushed the call button again. But no one had come and he'd had to crawl back to his bed, moaning with pain.

He would punch the Greyhound bus driver who wouldn't let him board. And all the salespeople who refused to wait on him. In the last few years he rarely traveled even to Sharon. Why suffer? In Paris he was known and respected. And if he stayed in Paris no one whispered or pointed or called him names.

He had developed routines. He bought his clothes from catalogs, always men's size small, and he took them to Mary, the seamstress, who cut the unneeded length from the sleeves and pant legs and sewed the cuffs back on so no one could tell they had been altered. A few times a year he left Paris to visit book dealers in New England, but he always drove and he didn't stop at restaurants or self-serve gas stations. The book dealers, even the ones who were meeting him for the first time, were the kind of people who appreciated the variations of life. And for them, until they got to know him, that's what he was. Then, when they knew him, they sometimes became friends. One man who lived in Massachusetts and had a three-story building filled with nothing but books said to him one evening when they were having dinner together, "You know, William, I always forget that you're a little bit shorter than most other people. To me, you're William Swick, the book dealer from New York, a guy I like spending time with."

"Thank you," William said. And he meant it. When he drove home from that trip, the back of the pick up filled with boxes of books, he'd heard it over and over. "You're William Swick, a guy I like spending time with." It was one of the kindest things anyone had ever said to him.

Until Uta. He wanted to marry his wide-hipped large-breasted, big-boned woman with the cheeks that turned red and chapped in the winter and the hands that kneaded bread dough as hard as she kneaded his skin when she was about to cry with pleasure. But would she even have this happy deluded sinner? Maybe she wanted to keep their sex life a secret.

So the first year passed. He would wait patiently through the days until the time he could be with her, when he spilled into her hand or onto her belly or deep into the darkness of her cavities and became completely known. Him, known. But it was true. His seed had settled inside, around, and on her body in so many agonies of passion he wanted to shout into the world: Hey you out there, the dwarf and the German are doing it! All's well on Eastern Road! In the big white house there's fucking!

Would she marry him? He was afraid to ask her. The second year passed. Helene turned into a woman. He remembered an evening when Gunter was lying in the living room building a city out of cardboard blocks. The noise was tremendous each time Gunter knocked the blocks over.

Helene was sitting at the table reading a book. Her thin straight hair curled down over the front of her sweater. After two years, she could read English as well as she could read German and she was concentrating on the book with all the intensity that a child who wants to be accepted brings to the activity that seems to promise success. It was a Girl Scout handbook. Uta didn't know what Girl Scouts were and William, in his blindness and preoccupation, didn't understand that Helene needed someone to drive her to the store and buy her a uniform. She wouldn't have asked. All matters of money he had to bring up himself. So once a year, he suggested they take the children shopping for clothes. Any extras beyond that—socks, notebooks, underwear—came out of his pocket, too. Helene took charge of the weekly household money as soon as she was old enough, but it was another year before he gave her that responsibility.

If only he could go back there. But in its greedy haste, time pushed on. And then, one night only a short while later, Helene was twenty-three and standing at the sink washing dishes. It was inexplicable. Nothing ever stayed still long enough for a person to get it down as completely and thoroughly as was necessary. If he could say, *Here, this is the place, let me just be here*, those were the weeks he would have chosen to remain in, starting with the evening Helene was washing the dishes and Gunter was outside splitting firewood. He wanted to go back there and get it right. Not about the Girl Scouts, the Girl Scouts had been forgotten, and in the end, it didn't make much difference that she had missed that one American activity. Others came along to take its place. But that night in the kitchen he was feeling brave enough to risk it all and ask Uta. Gunter was fifteen, still in high school. Every day he rode his bicycle the seven miles to school, and when he wanted to see friends in the village, no matter if it was raining or snowing, he biked there. He was tall and strong, a man of the elements. So even though it was dark and cold outside, Gunter was standing under the light at the back door chopping wood. He'd thrown off his jacket and stripped down to his T-shirt. Helene had just finished two years at the community college and started working at the post office. She had bought her own car with the money she had made working part-time at the drugstore in town, and was paying back her school loan. But now, with a full-time job, she wasn't at home very much, and with Gunter spending more and more time in the village with his friends, for most of the day Uta was alone.

"Villiam," Uta said, "every other voman has car."

"A car," he said gently, not because he cared whether she spoke properly or not, but because she had instructed him to correct her.

"Every other voman has a car. They don't have no fish at home for supper, they drive a car to buy a fish."

"Some fish," he said.

"They don't have no anything, what they make for dinner? Not vorry! Voman gets into a car and drive to buy a something."

"But, Uta, you're always prepared. You have chicken in the freezer, potatoes and carrots in the cold room. You have cabbages. You always have food. So that's a situation that will never happen to you."

She said something in German to Helene and Helene answered her back. Finally Uta sighed and looked at him.

"Not only a fish! A happiness at not being home! I have a happiness at not being home when I go out to buy a fish!"

"You don't even have to buy a fish," he said softly. "You can come into town to go to lunch or get a cup of coffee or visit me."

"Some car to do that is vat I like," she said. "For a fish or a happiness. Vith some car it vouldn't matter."

"A car is what you shall have then," William said. "But first, you have to learn how to drive."

"To drive I know," Uta said.

"She does," Helene volunteered, turning around to wipe her hands on a towel. "Mama drove Granddaddy's car."

"Why you never told me that! Uta, why did you keep it a secret that you can drive?"

She looked down at the floor, her cheeks red with embarrassment. "Twenty years ago, maybe I drive. Now I don't remember."

"It'll come back, Mama. Driving is like learning how to ride a bicycle. You'll see. It'll all come back. You never forget how to drive."

"But maybe I forget."

"No you won't, Mama. You'll surprise yourself."

It was then that William remembered the talking he had been hearing in the bathroom. He thought they were discussing women's things but now he saw that Uta had confided her loneliness and Helene had suggested a car. Why hadn't she come to him? If they were married, she would have known how much she meant to him and when she had a problem, she would ask his advice. All that time, thirteen years, she'd been cooking and keeping house and providing for all of them, and he had never once wondered if she was lonely. He just assumed that for her, too, the outside world held dangers. And maybe he liked having her always there. Maybe it pleased him to have that portion of his existence under control. Well, he would find her a big, safe, not-much-to-look-at car. And the other thing he would do was ask her to marry him.

By the end of the week he'd located a ten-year-old Ford station wagon. A friend who was a good customer as well as a mechanic checked it out and as an added favor drove it to the farmhouse and then hitched a ride back into town. Uta called him at the store. "Vat is that out there?"

"What is what out where?"

"Out vindow in garage."

"In the garage?"

"Some car! Some car has come in garage. For vat, Villiam? For vat is some car?"

"It's for a fish and a happiness. Did you forget?"

"For me?" she asked.

"For you because I love you. I love you so much I can't tell you."

"I vait until you come home to drive," she said and hung up.

Would she even have him if he asked her to marry him? She took a car so easily. Not even a thank-you. It was the same way she took his body and expected him to do likewise with hers. Though each time he wanted to get down on his knees and thank her. He had only given her a car. Could he also give her a ring and ask her to marry him? Or would that be different? Would she not want to bother with marriage the same way she didn't want to bother with thank-yous?

He wondered if he should ask Helene. She would know

how her mother felt. But he couldn't ask his lover's daughter to give him advice, particularly when she was his lover's only friend and confidante.

If the universe would pause, that would be the place he wanted to go back to because that was the closest he ever came. *Will you marry me?* It was going to be the next thing out of his mouth. He was ready and the phone offered the necessary protection; he wouldn't have to learn from her face that she thought the idea preposterous. But she hung up too quickly and over the months that followed, the business of getting her used to driving occupied the entire household. Helene gave her lessons. William gave her lessons. Gunter asked her to drive him to his friends' houses. But Uta was nervous. It took an entire year before she was confident enough to go out on her own. And even then, she would only drive if the roads were dry and the day was sunny, and she would only go to the village and back and only on one route, and if it started to snow when she was in town she'd panic and leave right away. One day, she came back from her weekly trip to the village and said, "People die in cars, Villiam, too fast they drive."

"Some people do drive too fast," he said, "but the other unsafe drivers are the ones who drive too slow." But he didn't tell her she ought to go faster because he could see her happiness, her flushed cheeks, her bright eyes, and he knew how proud she was to be able to go to town on her own.

So why hadn't he brought up the question in all the years that followed? Some night when she came to his room, before she tiptoed out early in the morning to feed the dog and the chickens and greet the day, why hadn't he just whispered in her ear, *Will you marry me?*

She wouldn't have answered right away because she wouldn't have known what the word meant. So then he would have had to explain it and while he did that he would have had to watch her face. He would have seen the moment when she understood, and the moment after that, he would have seen the answer, and he was scared because he had a feeling it wouldn't have been yes.

Twenty-Three

~⌒

*F*aith woke up in the middle of the night thinking about the phone call from William. That poor lonely little man. Of course she would have dinner with him on Friday. She'd have dinner with him any time he asked. She extended her foot out of the covers and searched with it along the floor until she felt her slipper. She settled her bare foot into its warm furry inside, picked her robe up from the empty side of her double bed, and walked through her dark apartment to the kitchen. She put the light on, poured milk into a saucepan, and put it on the stove to get warm. It was lack of calcium that caused her middle-of-the-night wakings and she treated it with one large cup of hot milk every morning at three A.M.

She thought about the day. After school got out, she would invite Stella to have a cup of coffee with her in town. They'd just talk for a while and then Faith would ask her about her home life and if it seemed really horrible, she could always offer Stella the spare room. There was a cry for help in that speech she gave to the class and Faith couldn't pretend she hadn't heard it.

It was a nice room. They could go to the paint store together and pick out a new color for it. She'd give Stella the spare bookcase in the living room and they'd bring up her old college desk from the basement so Stella would have a place to study. They'd discuss rules, like when it should be lights off, when it should be curfew. Money they would have to figure out. Faith was prepared to support Stella, even pay for paint and curtains and a fancy new bedspread, but maybe Stella would feel better if it wasn't all so easy. What if Faith asked for one day a week of major housecleaning and they each did their own laundry? In the spring they'd go around together and look at colleges. Stella was a smart girl. She wouldn't have any problem getting a scholarship.

Of course there was the nasty little matter of sex. Darryl was a nice kid, but a boy after all, and what if Stella got pregnant? Whose responsibility would it be then? Maybe the first thing Faith should do was send her to the clinic for birth control. Only that was a moral issue and maybe the mother would take exception. But maybe she wouldn't, and anyway, how would she know? So, no boys in Stella's room. That she'd have to make clear. No parties, no making-out, not there. One thing she would have to be very careful about was Lucille. Lucille would have to stay in Sharon for the next six months. One glance at her would wreck it all.

She caught the milk before it boiled and poured the hot frothy liquid into her cup. She sprinkled some cinnamon and sugar on the top, then took it out to the dark living room and sat on the couch. She dialed Lucille's number by the light coming in through the curtains, let it ring once, and hung up. If Lucille was awake, she would call back. And she might be because on Thursdays her shift went until two A.M. The phone chimed softly. "Hey, sweet," Faith whispered. "You're still up?"

"I just got home. Having some dinner."

"What'd you make?"

"My usual Thursday-night stuff, eggs and home fries. What's going on with you? Why are you awake?"

"I'm worried."

"Well, everything's fine with me and I love you more than ever and the world is okay."

"I was thinking about Stella."

"The dark-haired one with the lousy home life?"

"That's her. Well..." Faith described the speech Stella had given in class and Lucille said, "Good thing she's smart, isn't it?"

"She's not brilliant. She just seems very sensible and aware."

"Well, that's good. Otherwise she could really head down the wrong road."

"I want to help her."

There was silence. Lucille worked at a residence for troubled teenagers. She maintained that the only way she had stayed there for eleven years was by teaching herself not to bring the kids' lives home with her.

"I'm not trying to save her. She doesn't need saving, and I think I'm smarter than that anyway. I just want to talk to her and if things seem really bad, offer her room and board in exchange for one day a week of housecleaning."

"That's a pretty good deal. If I were in her situation, I'd move in tomorrow."

"There's only one thing."

"Me," Lucille said. "Faith, what does it always come down to? You've chosen to live here. I've chosen to live here. And it's not San Francisco. But I can't exist if I have to hide. So I say who I am and anybody doesn't like it, they get out of my way. I don't give them my power. I keep it for myself. You're giving control to these other people, Faith. You've got to keep it for yourself. I'm not talking about flaunting anything. I'm just talking about living your life without tiptoeing around. Do you know what I mean?"

"I wish I could be as brave about it as you are."

"You can. It's easy. Look in the mirror. Take power from that face looking back at you. You can even try something, okay? Take your hands and touch your face really softly and gently. Tell yourself, *You are so beautiful, you are so lovely. I love you so much.* Keep on stroking and caressing. *Oh, I love you so much.* Feel your cheekbone. Feel your forehead. Close your eyes and feel your eyeballs. Something'll happen. It'll come up into your hands."

Lucille didn't go on. "What happens?" said Faith. "What comes into your hands?"

"Don't you know, woman? Are you so separate from your body that you can't tell me?"

"Well, I guess it's some sense of yourself. Some kind of acceptance."

"That's what you might think, sure," said Lucille. "You've been punishing yourself for so long, acceptance looks really good to you. It looks like it's the final prize. No, it's more than that."

"You know I don't like this sensitivity training stuff. And

I'm probably not going to do it," Faith said. "So you might as well tell me."

"This would be so good for you. Because you know what comes up, woman, your soul. It's your soul you'll feel rising into your hands. Your ancient, wise, tired and battered soul. It's your child and it wants to be noticed and cared for."

"I don't know."

"I know you don't know, sweetheart. It ain't Shakespeare. But if you want my opinion, Shakespeare was a woman. Listen, I gotta go finish my supper."

Twenty-Four

~~~

Uta Hugel sat in the bomb shelter of her small apartment building wrapped in a blanket. Helene was beside her wearing a dress and party shoes under her winter coat. With ribbons in her hair and the little patent-leather purse she held in her lap, she looked as though she were on her way to someone's birthday celebration. In truth, she had just come home from a party she had gone to with her mother. Uta had been changing out of her good clothes when the sirens went off, which was why she'd put on the first things she'd pulled out of her closet, a skirt and an old moth-eaten sweater. She still wore her good silk stockings, the ones Wolff had brought back for her from France, but she'd had time to put on her comfortable shoes.

Sitting with them in the shelter were Herr Steinbach and Frau Metzger, both from the third floor. The Singers, who had lived on the first floor, had been taken away one afternoon when Uta hadn't been home. They were Jewish. The couple who had moved in afterwards, whose names she could never remember, had gone to the country, and Herr Dunkel, from the second floor like her, was in the hospital.

Usually, the planes hit the railroad yards at the other side of the city and went away. The all clear would sound and the feeling of dread would suddenly lift and everyone would start talking. But this time the all clear didn't sound and the bombs were getting closer. There were many times when she thought they were finished but then a plane came over again. One explosion was so loud she was sure it had hit their building. Uta pulled Helene onto her lap and wrapped the blanket around her. It was clear that the entire city was being destroyed and nothing that they believed in was of any consequence. There was no meaning at all. No sense. Her life, her daughter's life...the building would collapse and if her friends and relatives had perished as well, no one would be alive to count their absence. All of their importance suddenly nothing. She could hear a fire roaring outside. It would burn her remains. Maybe all that would be left would be a few tortoise shell hairpins that someone many years later would find in the ashes. No sense. She started to sing to Helene, but softly so that the others couldn't hear. It was a children's song about a rooster and a donkey bragging over who could sing better to welcome in the spring. Spring would still come because it was February four-teenth already. Even with all this agony. The tune took hold of her. The words came around over and over as the buildings tumbled outside. Even down in the basement, she could hear the wind starting up.

When it seemed that the bombing had stopped, Herr Steinbach and Frau Metzger, ages seventy and seventy-two, decided to stay where they were and wait for the rescue crews. Uta was afraid their building would collapse as soon as the roof caught on fire, which would happen quickly because the bombs had been close. She took two pairs of goggles, one for Helene, one for herself, and adjusted each pair to fit over their heads. The blankets and the goggles had been supplied by Frau Metzger, who had been through a bombing raid in Hamburg and knew what was necessary.

Uta wet her blanket in the tub of water that Frau Metzger kept in the shelter for that purpose and, wrapping it around Helene and herself, climbed the stairs to the door at the top. She was still singing the song. She opened the door, then closed it tightly behind her. As soon as she stepped into the foyer, she could hear the fires roaring outside. She opened the door onto the street and stepped into a hot red wind. Glass rained down around their blanket-wrapped bodies. Chairs flew past them. A man bumped into her. He had a bloody face and he was holding a dead child in his arms. Uta pushed past him, leaning into the wind. She decided to cut through the park. She bent her head down, pulled the wet blanket around her sweating shoulders, pulling it over Helene's hair, and tried to see through the wind. It pushed her backwards, but she walked into it and tunneled through, still singing the song.

Kuckuck, kuckuck, kuckuck, kuckuck,
Iiiaaa, Iiiaaa
Wer wohl am besten sänge
zur schönen Maienzeit
Kuckuck, kuckuck, kuckuck, kuckuck,
Iiiaaa, Iiiaaa

Wer wohl am besten sänge
zur schönen Maienzeit

With her head pressed against Uta's chest, Helene heard enough of the song to sing the animal sounds with Uta: *kuckuck, kuckuck, iiiaaa, iiiaaa*...No one else seemed to be moving with any purpose. They went past so many dead bodies, past screaming dying bodies, past shoes and arms, past a headless girl hanging from a burning tree, that none of it seemed unusual. It was the simple and uncomplicated end of the world and Uta felt she was a dead person already, only she was walking and happened to be carrying a child and singing a song. As soon as she reached the park she knew she couldn't walk through it. The ground was heaped with bodies, the agonies of suffocation on their faces. The trees were hung with furniture, drapery, body parts. She took the long way around, walking down one red windy street after another. Her voice against the roaring fires was very faint, but she kept singing. When she was too tired to walk, she lay down in the remains of a building, holding Helene close to her. They slept for a few hours and woke up to a morning that was dark and sooty. When the smoke cleared, she started out again. After hours of walking, holding the child's hand, she came to a road that went into the country and there she saw other people escaping the city as she was. She talked to no one. She sang the song over and over.

In the afternoon they came to a refugee camp where an official was signing in a group of exhausted-looking people. She knew what happened in those places. The Mongolian soldiers who were coming into Germany ahead of the Russians tore through those camps, raping and stealing. The official told her she must sign in, she could go no further, but Uta, who kept Helene hidden under the blanket, sneaked past him when he was detained with a man who was badly burned, and kept on walking. When she saw a train waiting at an outlying station she didn't get on it because it would be an easy target for enemy planes. She ducked into a grove of trees and spread her blanket on the ground. Helene was too frightened to speak and just curled up next to her. Uta pulled her coat around them and, huddled together, they slept through the next day and that night started walking again.

For five days they walked, sleeping in ditches, behind buildings, under trees. It was cold. Uta broke through the ice in streams so they could have water. Bits of food that Uta found she gave to Helene. They walked all the way into the foothills on the eastern border of Germany. It started to snow. For Uta it was a blessing, this water that came down from the sky so kindly, that it could douse any fire, quench any thirst. She ate it and showed Helene how to eat it but they were too cold and wet to continue and it was already night. In the darkness, they discovered a pile of soft earth. It gave off a tremendous heat and they burrowed into it, pushing the earth on top of them so they were completely buried in its warmth. It was the first time in many days that they slept deeply. All through the night Uta was aware of a rich smell that she couldn't identify. In the morning when she heard the sound of a farmer rattling by in his hay wagon, she scrambled to her feet and waved him down. She went back to get Helene and then she saw what they had been sleeping in. It was a pile of manure. It gave off so much heat, steam spiraled up from it into the cold air.

For two days they rode in the farmer's wagon, lying in the

sweet-smelling hay. He crossed into Czechoslovakia, taking them into the mountains. Then they were on foot again. When they came into a small village, Uta knocked on a door and asked if she could have some food and water for herself and her child. A woman invited them inside and gave them a loaf of bread and milk to drink. She wanted to know where they were going, where they came from. Uta told her Dresden and the woman laughed.

"No one survived Dresden. Everyone was killed there. You are crazy if you think I would believe you came all the way from Dresden, and with a child that young."

Uta asked her if she knew the song about the rooster and the donkey bragging over who could sing better to welcome in the spring.

The woman said of course she did.

Uta told her that she'd been singing that song for six days as she walked, and in all of that time the animals hadn't stopped arguing. Maybe the world had fallen apart, but those two stupid animals were keeping the two of them alive.

The woman gave Uta a mug of beer and said, "If you came from Dresden, I will give you my own bed to sleep in tonight, and fresh clothes to wear tomorrow, and I will serve you a big breakfast, and I will pack a lunch for you. I will boil water for you and your daughter to bathe in. I will kill my fattest rooster for you to eat. If you came from Dresden..." The woman in the village didn't have anything else to offer so she simply put her hand over Uta's hand and then, in a burst of feeling, pulled Uta towards her roughly and threw her big arms around such a miracle.

Twenty-Five

*T*he first word went across. It was *havoc*. The second word went down. It was *vein*. The third word was *ink*. That was his. Because it was only three letters he pulled off his T-shirt. She stared at his nipples. When it was her turn, she put *p* onto *ink*. He wrote *kick*. She made *kiss*. He put an *o* under the *s* and took off his pants. His undershorts were pale blue, a color he said he hated. She added *n-l-y* to the *o* in *so* to make *only*. He added *i-t* to make *nit* and pulled off his boxers.

She wondered if he was making short words on purpose. "It's clear who's the better Scrabble player, isn't it?"

"Maybe so, maybe not. Your turn."

She settled her eyes on his beautiful genital fruit. Then she made *tank*. He wrote *kind*. She put an *o* next to the *d*, not because she felt sorry for him, but because it was, literally, all she could think of. What to take off? She wasn't wearing socks or a bra, but at least she was wearing underpants so she wriggled out of her jeans. He added *o-r* to her *do* to make *door* and all of a sudden she said, looking down at her tiles, "Wow! I don't believe what I've got here." She put *a-r-i-s* next to the *P* and made *Paris*.

"Hey, cool!"

In one way, he looked perfectly reasonable in his nakedness. But in the other, it was all she could do to sit there, his body speaking to her fingers, her tongue, talking out loud to her own body, breast to breast, leg to leg. The flowers in her mouth had popped up and noticed.

He said, "You can't use names."

"You can't?"

"You can't."

"Who says?"

"It's the rules."

"Let's change the rules."

"You can't change the rules."

"You can," she said. "I do it every day."

"I don't care if you do it every day or once a week. You can't change the rules. Look, I'm lying over here freezing and you're sitting there with most of your clothes on arguing with me."

"You can change the rules because if you couldn't, you wouldn't get anywhere."

"Okay, names are allowed from now on." He put *n-d-y* onto the *i*.

"What's that?"

"It's the name of a famous car race."

"*Indy?*"

"Yeah. Everyone knows it. It's very famous."

She put all of her letters after *Paris* and made a thirteen-letter word that covered a triple word space.

"What the hell is that?"

"That's the name of something."

"Oh yeah, what?"

"It's the name of something that you do when you live in Paris and you want something that you know you won't ever have. You *shalagog* it."

"So it's a verb."

"Yeah, shalagoging is an action. Parisshalagoging is shalagoging that's done in Paris."

"As opposed to Sharonshalagoging?"

"You can't shalagog in Sharon. You can only do it in Paris. This is the only place where everything is right for it."

"You're making it up."

"I'm not."

"You are. You're a sore loser."

"And you have no imagination. And you might think you have a lot of imagination because you dream up this thing about flowers in my mouth, but really, when it comes down to it, you don't understand anything. Because my imagination is the way that I live. I don't save it for paintings. I live it every day because if I didn't I wouldn't have anything." She could feel her eyes getting wet, but she ignored it. "And you don't know anything about that because you have everything you need and you've always had it. I don't know about paintings like you do, and I don't know the names of famous artists or famous car races, but imagination is something I'm very familiar with because I imagine how to get a wardrobe out of three lousy shirts and two lousy pairs of pants. And I imagine how to get dinner out of low-fat cottage cheese and diet soda. I imagine it."

He put up his hand. "Okay, okay, you do. And that's what I love about you. You imagine your entire existence. Much more than I do. But this is Scrabble and Scrabble has rules and one of the rules is that the words have to mean something. So I don't buy your line about Parisshalagoging."

"Buy is a good way to put it."

"Sssh," he whispered, and put his finger over his mouth. "I think I heard something." They were quiet. His room was off the main part of the house so it was unlikely anyone had heard them.

When they were sure the silence was as dense and thick as before, she went on, but in a whisper. "All you know is extremes. Buy and sell. Love and hate. Black and white. That's how you think. You ignore anything that isn't big and loud."

"Such as?"

"Parisshalagoging." She wanted to shake him, make him open his eyes. But instead she said quietly, "Which is what you can do here because this is the only place in the world where the air has the right density and the water has the right minerals and the soil has the right mixture of whatever and things that can't be attempted anywhere else can be done here. So there's much more than buying and selling and getting dressed and getting undressed and loving someone and hating someone in Paris." She reached for her jeans.

He put his hand on her arm. "Hey!"

"Hey yourself!"

"You really want to put those back on?"

"Maybe."

"But maybe not." He scooted over to her so that his bare flesh finally touched her bare flesh. Then he lifted her T- shirt and sank his face into her chest.

She lay down. He breathed against her, his nose brushing against her stomach. She took his head in her hands and scooted down flat so they were face to face, breast to breast. She was going to shalagog him. In all need, in all hunger, and simply because he was all she had.

Later, they crept down the thickly carpeted hallway, past the bathroom, past the closed door of his parents' room, the closed door of his sister's room, down the stairs, nothing ever creaking as they tiptoed through the well-made house. He pulled the front door open and she was out alone in the night. She said, "Fuck" under her breath. Fuck, fuck, fuck, fuck. Damn. She could be so exasperated with him and love him so much, all at the same time.

As she walked down the sidewalk she realized she knew some things. She didn't know them in a fashion she could repeat to someone else, she simply understood them like she understood her mother, who was a white person through and through but still lived outside of a rational structure the way people of color did. She had a job, but that was about as far as it went. The rest of her life was a bright, glittering spiral that traveled down and down, always pausing at the same little particle of resentment, which was Stella's father.

What she knew about Darryl was sex. It was the only thing she could give him. Her skin, her flowers, her hair as black as night. She was better than his dreams. He lost himself, got tangled up, but she stayed alert and watchful. Only when it all checked out, when she was sure the silence in the house was total, did she let herself go for her own moment of feeling. Only then.

It was three in the morning. The moon was round and bright and far away. Where did a woman go who was half-Mexican in a white town and had thighs sticky from lovemaking with the son of the doctor? She opened her sweater and let the air brush past her. She shook out her hair and started to run down the sidewalk, feeling his juice spill into her underpants. A dog from deep inside one of the houses called out to her. How far could she walk? Until light, probably, and then she could hitch a ride on the highway and disappear. No. She had to stay in Paris because she couldn't manage anywhere else. The air was right, the soil was right, the water was right. On Main Street, which was soft and peaceful looking, she stopped running and started to skip. She swung her arms side to side to the rhythm, her hair whipping around, her bag banging against her shins. There were stacks of newspapers outside Smokes and Jokes and a light on in a room over Better Days. She turned into the alley and skipped past the dumpsters and garbage cans, around the no-parking signs. She frightened a cat, which streaked across the dirt in front of her, then she stopped at an unmarked door and pulled it open, leaving it open so the moonlight would illuminate the stairway, and climbed up.

At the top, she opened the next door and turned on the light. One day this empty room was going to be her lover's studio. She'd pose for him. Maybe in the long red dress they'd found up here in a box. Maybe naked. She walked over to the closet and standing on tiptoe, felt on top of the molding for the key. She opened the door. The old ledgers from Baldwin Mercantile were stored in there along with a couple of ancient cash registers as well as the red velvet dress. She pulled off her T-shirt, stepped out of her pants, tossed her underpants on top of the pile, and pulled the garment over her head. It almost fit her, but the neckline was a little too low and the dress, which stopped at her ankles, was a little short. It didn't matter. She was strange and elegant anyway. Pushing the hangers and boxes and piles of magazines over to the walls, she cleared the space. Then she lifted her skirt and twirled around, her eyes on the painting Darryl had pinned to the wall. One enormous green apple filling up an entire room. That guy Magritte knew how to shalagog. Maybe the man sitting at his kitchen table in the building across the way did, too. Why else would he be awake at this hour? She swayed back and forth in front of the window. Then she put her hands over her head and moved about in a private dance she could feel growing up inside her. She turned back to the window and looked. The guy was slumped over like he had fallen asleep. What if she slipped out of the dress and danced naked? No, the only person she would show her body to was Darryl, old black-and-white, love-and-hate, dressed-and-undressed Darryl. Maybe it was the privilege of a guy who grew up with everything plentiful and in easy reach to ignore the in-between areas, the almosts and not-quites.

She tried the window because she wanted to let night in and it opened easily. Poking her head outside, she noticed the ledge that ran below the window and ended in steplike bricks that made a stairway to the roof, which was the last stop, she realized, before the moon. She might dance naked for the moon. She might show the moon her perfect body so the moon would come down to her. She put one bare leg out of the window. She hiked her skirt up and sat on the windowsill, both legs hanging outside. She might call the moon down to the roof and demand an explanation. Why did she live up here in this place of white snow and white people when she could be down there where it was hot and brown? She stood up on the ledge, which was just wide enough to hold her feet. She turned around. The bricks were angled at the right place for her hands. She inched along the ledge, belly flat against the building, her pelvis brushing along the ancient brick. Two floors below her, a car passed down the street, the driver no doubt shalagoging just as she was because who else would be out at that hour? Only the ones who had holes in their lives and had to sneak around in this rational place, corner to corner, hallway to hallway, nighttime to nighttime, collecting the things they needed and didn't quite ever get. At last, her stairway to the moon. The clock on the bank said 4:07. The temperature was forty-three degrees. She placed a foot on the first brick. It moved. Oh God, it was sitting there looking like it was cemented in but it was loose! She inched over and felt one of the bricks on top. Steady, steady. Just that one brick was loose. The rest didn't move. She hung on with her hands and climbed up one little brick at a time, and at the top, stepped down onto the flat empty roof. It stretched out to the end of the world with nothing on any of the sides to prevent her from slipping off.

But she wouldn't. She was strong and surefooted and beautiful. Oh yes, she was beautiful. She pulled the dress over her head and flung it down. She would be naked for the moon. Then she turned around to the soft breeze that invited her to move with it. Below her, where she couldn't see, the time on the bank changed. Up here, away from its jurisdiction, the night was chaos, the future and past streaming by with the present so the air was thick and sensuous. She danced to Main Street, to the seven orbs of light from the seven street lamps, to the yellow window across the way where the same man who had been asleep leaned out of his window and waved his arms at her. She couldn't hear what he was saying. The only sound up there was the turning of the earth, which spun on its axis so slowly it hardly counted as anything at all.

She danced to Darryl, to his hands and mouth, to his future. She was going to have his babies. She danced to herself in the future when she would be old and heavy and tired of babies. Would she still have flowers in her mouth? She would have become flowers entirely, fully open and fragrant. Nothing would scare her then. The sky sat over her, its legs spread like a great hungry woman and after a while, far away in the East, she saw the opening at the center. It was shy at first, just a little blush, but then it started to pulse and throb as tongues of red licked up from the horizon. She hummed. She swayed. She moved in great wide circles, feet kicking up, hair swinging. Then she began to glide. One Two Three, One Two Three. The music went on and on, ruffling up the breeze. The breeze was her partner and they circled the roof, back and forth, side to side, kicking and swaying, galloping. Then it was over. The night was turning violet. Day was peeking out. She curtsied. The breeze bowed. She picked her dress up from the roof and pulled it over her head. It stuck to her hot sweaty skin. The man across the way was watching her. A person could dance at night on top of a roof. She wasn't disturbing anyone. So what was the problem? She walked over to the edge to try to hear what he was saying.

"What're you doing up there?"

"I'm getting down," she called.

"Don't do anything! Wait! Everything's all right! I'll be

right there! Hold on! Just hold on!"

When he disappeared from the window, she thought he was at the phone, calling the police. But then he was running across the street, waving and shouting at her.

"I'm not going to jump," she called down to him. "I'm just going to climb down. It's okay. I came out of the window."

"Hey, kid, whatever your name is, that's not a smart thing to do!"

"It's easy!" she called as she walked to the edge. She put one foot down onto the stairway and then another, but as she put the second one down, the brick she was holding onto with her hand broke off and she grabbed the edge of the roof. The brick under her foot was shifting under the sudden weight. It was the loose one. She tried to toe it back into place but she pushed it too far and it fell out, taking the bricks below it, too, so that underneath her feet there was yawning space. When they hit the pavement there should have been a shattering noise. But she didn't hear it; there was a noise in her ears instead, a crackling sound.

"Hold on! I'm calling the firemen. Hold on!"

She couldn't. Her fingers were sliding in the crumbly stuff on the roof and there was nothing for her feet to rest on. The crackling grew louder. She heard his voice from somewhere else now. He must have gone up to his apartment to telephone.

"They're coming, hold on!"

She couldn't. She started to cry.

"Hold on!" His voice was closer. She shook her head to clear out the noise. He was below her now. "Hold on, sweetheart!"

She opened and shut her mouth a few times to clear her head. There were two inches of roof to slide through until she

got to the little lip on the edge. Two inches until the end of her
life. "I can't," she cried out, her voice echoing down the length
of the street. The crackling inside her head had stopped and
silence swelled in her brain. Never before had it been so quiet.
She cried out, "I'm sliding off."

"Listen, baby..." He sounded tired. "I know you're sliding.
I'm going to hold you up. Listen. Slide slowly. Slow down. The
truck's coming. They got my call. But the guys have to get to the
station first. It'll be maybe fifteen minutes. I'm going to hold
you up. Listen, sweetheart. This is a crazy thing you were doing,
but the ladder's coming. You'll be taken care of. But it's going
to be a few minutes so you'll have to hold on. Listen, slow
down. I know you're sliding, but slow down. I love you. I love
you because you're doing this crazy thing. Yeah, he loves me,
you think. The dirty old man. That's not what I mean. You're
not alone. You get me? We have each other."

She bumped down a notch as her fingers scraped through
the gravel on the roof. The clock on the bank was below her.
She could hear it click when the minute changed.

"Whatever your name is up there, you have this wild streak
that I know about. But it'll get you in trouble."

She knew, she knew. Her fingers were sliding and she couldn't
slow them down.

"Hold on, the ladder's coming!"

She sobbed. He said, "Shut up! Save your energy for grabbing
on. Grab onto that sucker up there. I see lights at the end of the
street. Maybe it's a fire truck.... It's a car, but maybe the next one
will be your ladder."

"Call my mother," she said into the brick. She lifted her head.
She was so exhausted. "Call my mother!" she shouted. It was

more than she could manage. She put her face into the wall.

"Okay, you stay there. What's your number?"

"No! I'll fall! Please! Stay!" She would let go if he wasn't down there with her.

"All right, baby, I'm here. I'm not going no place. Who's your mother?"

"No talking!" she cried. Talking was such an effort. "Don't let me fall. Stay, please, stay, please, stay, please, don't slip." She whispered to her hands, "Stay, stay, stay." She slid down another inch and he saw it.

"Goddamn it, we're not playing games here. Now hold on!"

"Stay!" she commanded her fingers, which ached all the way up to her arms. Dropping down to the earth would be such a relief. Just to say, Please tell my mother I love her but I can't hold on any more, and then simply let go and tumble gracefully down through the air. How would she look crumpled down on the ground? Would Darryl weep?

"You hear that siren? That's for you, baby. The whole world's coming out for you. We're going to take care of you. Give you breakfast. Buy you clothes. Whatever you want, sweetheart. All doors in this town will be open to you. We love you, sweetheart. Whatever your name is, we're going to take care of you."

She slid down another inch.

"Ten more seconds. Come on, baby, you can give me that."

But she couldn't. Her arms were numb. Her fingers weren't gripping any longer. There wasn't any sensation in her feet either. She was just a long awkward thing ready to flop down to the pavement. It would be part of the same dance. She would do it gracefully. Maybe she wouldn't even fall. Maybe she would let go and then drop down on currents of air slowly, leisurely, just like a bird. Why hadn't she thought about that before? There wasn't any reason to hurt so much. She would simply spiral down and land on her feet. So when her hands gave way, when her fingers straightened out, and her arms fell down to her sides, she wouldn't panic. She would remember that she was as empty as air and was only returning to the place where she came from. Life hadn't filled her up at all. He hadn't filled her up. She was so empty she would float. She started to pull all thought out of her fingers.

Underneath her, the siren stopped. In a dream she heard him say, "There's a big red truck here and right as I speak there's a ladder moving up and a net..."

"Stay where you are," a voice commanded her through a loudspeaker. "Don't move."

"Okay kid," another voice said right behind her. "I'm going to put my arms around you and lift you off..."

But she wanted to float. She wanted to go down on her own to show them how weightless and graceful she was. None of life's grime had touched her. She was as clean and chaste as a bird. Arms in a rubber coat gripped her and lifted her up. Her feet were placed on the metal rungs of a ladder and a body stood behind her, steadying her arms. She started to shake.

"Just step down, one rung at a time. It's a long way and we're going to do it slowly. Be careful. I don't want you to trip."

She was shaking so violently he moved in closer. "Kind of cold for no jacket, ain't it?" She couldn't talk.

When they got to the bottom, she was passed to the man. Someone wrapped a blanket around her. She felt the warmth but she couldn't stop shaking. He said, "You're coming up to my apartment to get warm. One of these gentlemen will follow us up. He has some questions to ask you, but it's nothing to worry about. You're safe now, okay?" He put his arm around her shoulder, but she crumpled against him and he held her like that, right on the sidewalk, in full view of all the people driving to work.

Their footsteps on the stairway going up to his apartment were thunderous. The man cleared things off his table and they all sat down. He wiped up a puddle of food in front of her. The policeman took out a notebook and asked her for her name, the name of her parents or guardians, and the address and phone number where she lived, but she couldn't speak. The man, who was big and pasty looking, took her hand and held it in his own and his thick red fingers around her thin brown ones made her start to remember. The radiance started to drain out of her and the gray soot of the world sifted down before her eyes and filled in the empty spaces. With the police-man looking at her, too, sensation came back into her body. Memory returned and with it the dull ache of herself and the familiar throb of her name, her mother's name, and the name of the street she lived on. She couldn't tell them any numbers. Her phone number, her house number, and her age were still missing. Maybe there was that much of the radiance still left inside her. The man asked her to try to remember, but she knew that to pin herself down to a spot on the earth in the same way everyone else was pinned down would make it all disappear. So she held on to the little bit of weightlessness she could still feel inside her and shook her head.

"She's in shock," the man told the officer. "I'll get the information and call you later."

The policeman stood up, jangled the keys in his pocket. "She has to come to the station. We have to write up a report. Her mother will have to be notified."

"Her mother's sleeping," Harry said. "Her mother and I are old friends. Let her stay here and I'll call you up later with the information."

"I can't do that. Either she goes to the hospital or she comes with me to the station."

"She's a kid. Come on, Buddy, you and I were kids once. Remember that time you dove off the hilltop into the quarry? You could have hit your head on a rock. Did anyone take you down to the station? This is not a criminal act. Don't treat her like a criminal."

"All right, all right." The policeman named Buddy was backing out the door. "Give her some breakfast or something. Make sure she's warm enough. I'll be back in an hour."

"You doing okay?" the man called Harry asked when the policeman was gone. "Would you like to have a nap and some breakfast here, and then I can take you home when your mother's awake? Would you believe it's only six-thirty? You still shaking? Maybe it's hunger. Here, have something to eat."

She didn't want any of the greasy food she used to like. She wanted seeds and grass and crunchy uncooked things. She would like a carrot.

She looked at his wrinkled flannel shirt as he set a box of doughnuts on the table. He wore soft-looking corduroy pants. "They're fresh. I got them last night." Just to show her, he took one out for himself and bit into it. "Jelly filled." Syrup oozed over his lips and the smell of sugar broke into the room. It caused her stomach to rise and before she could stop herself, she was retching into the box. Darryl's mother's lasagna spilled out with bits of broccoli floating around the tomato sauce and cheese.

"Stay there," the man said, clattering out of his chair. "Don't move." He pulled a hunk of paper towels off a roll and gave her one to wipe her face while he mopped the stuff on the table. She noticed how careful he was not to let any of it touch him.

"I'm sorry," she mumbled, and although she didn't mean to, she started to cry because she could tell everything had left her. She knew numbers again, even the numbers of the combination lock on her locker at school. She herself had changed. She was thick and pasty, just like he was. Ordinary. She had Darryl's dried come in her panties. And now, to add to everything else, she smelled like vomit.

Twenty-Six

*O*f all the tricks the world could play, to be the one who rescued Hattie Doyle's daughter. What an old fart he was. He held the trash can at the edge of the table and wiped the mess into it. Then he realized she was sitting there crying and he was cleaning up like a goddamn housewife, not paying attention. "That's good enough," he said cheerfully. He threw the wad of paper towels away and put the trash can back under the sink. Her shoulders were hunched over, her hair hung in her face, and she wouldn't look up.

He cleared his throat. "I know what would feel real good to you right now. How 'bout a hot bath?" She sniffled and then stood up and he showed her to the bathroom. While the water was running until it became hot, he tried to neaten things. The clutter on the sink he grabbed and stuck into the medicine cabinet. Then he remembered the bathtub and knelt down to take a few swipes at the ring left there from the day before. He didn't want to scrub too vigorously; that would loosen the other older grime and it would be a half-an-hour session with cleanser, which he didn't think was necessary. It looked good enough so he put the plug in and let her fill. In the bedroom he found some towels and a pair of long johns that would be much too big, but would at least keep her warm. She'd closed the door so he knocked, then he opened it a crack, and handed them inside.

In the bedroom, Harry put fresh sheets on the bed and found an old wool blanket to substitute for the fur, which he pulled off and draped over a stack of boxes in the corner. He took a pair of worn boxer shorts from the bottom of his closet, where he stashed his dirty clothes until he found time to go to the laundromat, and used them to dust all of the surfaces. The kid was so tired she wouldn't notice. But he would feel better knowing it was a clean room she slept in. With drying her hair and whatever else she did, he assumed that the whole process of the bath and the nap would take maybe an hour. So she'd be ready by the time Buddy returned. Meanwhile, the kitchen was a mess. He was embarrassed that she had seen it. He ran soapy water into the sink and collected all of the dishes from the living room. Some were caked with weeks-old stew or eggs. He emptied the ashtrays and washed them out, too.

"Hey!"

She was calling. He went to the bathroom door. "My name is Harry."

"That's what I thought that policeman called you."

He could hardly hear her over the running water.

"Would you happen to be the Harry who owns the bar?"

"The same one. You need soap?" He hoped he had an extra bar of soap somewhere.

"No."

"What do you need?"

"Nothing. I just wanted to know if you were that Harry."

"Well, I am. What's the difference?"

She said, "You really are a friend of my mother's, aren't you?"

"Yeah, we go way back."

"Go ahead, you can open the door."

He thought of her ripe little body. "I have dishes to do. Take your bath." He started to walk away when she called out again. "Don't you want to come in? Come in, Harry, it's all right with me. I don't care."

The little flirt. He came back to the door and said, "Stella, you ought to protect yourself a little better."

"You sound like my grandfather."

"Well, sorry, kid, I didn't mean to."

"It's okay. Actually, my grandfather died a long time ago."

"What I mean is, it's not so smart to be like that. Don't come on to older men. Got it?" He cleared his throat. "You got to make choices. Have the courage to make some choices. Listen to me, an old fart telling you to have courage. After what you've been through. But courage applies to more than climbing on roofs. Save yourself for the things that really mean something. You understand?"

She didn't answer. He wasn't sure she was even listening.

"Stella, I'm not going to open this door. You don't come outta there till you got some clothes on, understand? You gotta take care of yourself. And if you're not going to do it...well, enough of the lecture. Take your bath."

When she walked out finally, her hair was dripping onto the shoulders of his enormous shirt. He realized he didn't even have a comb to offer her. "They sell combs down at Smokes?" he asked.

"I never comb it," she said. "I just let it dry and then I brush it." She sat on his couch and rubbed her hair with the towel while he rummaged around in his bedroom and came out with a pair of clean socks. "Here, put these on. They'll keep your feet warm."

"You're really nice to me, Harry."

"Well, everything I said to you when you were hanging down from that roof over there, it's all still true."

"Could we do something?"

"Like?"

"Like, could I just lie down here on your couch? Could I have a blanket and pillow and could we just talk and then maybe I'll be able to fall asleep?"

"Make yourself at home. You'll find what you need in the bedroom. I'm just going to go out on the landing and have a cigarette."

"You don't have to smoke out there for me," she said. "My mom smokes all the time in our house."

"Well, I'll just be a few minutes."

When he came back, she was on the couch, a blanket pulled up to her chin. He thought she might be asleep so he closed the door softly. But no, a thin little voice said, "You know how many years I've been hearing about Harry? I bet my mom owes you some money, doesn't she?"

"Don't recall. I'd have to check my book and my book is downstairs. Your mom, when she owes me, she pays up."

"That's good. I was asking because she never seems to have much money at home, but I guess she pays her bill at your place so she can come back. She likes your place a lot."

The way she looked at him made him want to move around a bit. So he got up and said, "What you mean is maybe she likes it too much."

"Maybe. So, when did you first meet my mother?"

He stopped fiddling around with the dishes and turned to face her even though those eyes of hers scared him a little. "Hattie and I, we go back to the beginning. She had her twenty-first birthday in my bar. My bar, listen to me, I was hardly older than she was. I just worked weekends. Was going to be ten years before I bought the place. I knew your mother before she knew your dad, who came onto the scene shortly after that birthday."

"You knew my father too?"

"I threw him out of the bar once for getting rough with someone. It wasn't that he was a rough man, he just didn't understand that you have to be different with women. He had a little problem with that. When was the last time you saw your daddy?"

"I was five, I think."

"Well, it's not your fault. He's just the kind of guy that never sticks around in one place too long. He thought women were just like men. And that you elbowed your way into a woman's life the same way you elbowed your way into a card game or a hunting trip. By always being there. He wouldn't let your mother go sometimes. Had to have her. She was pretty, blond curly hair, a cute figure. You got your dark looks from your dad. And something else too, I think. Your dad would have climbed up onto that roof. Course, your mother hasn't had an easy life. How's that car of hers doing? Still running?"

"Sort of," Stella said.

"She ever tell you it was me who located that car for her? Saw it in the paper and I says to myself, Hattie's looking for a car and she'd like a big pink one I bet. She looks good in it, don't you think?"

"I don't know," Stella said.

Well, that was right. Hattie didn't look good in anything anymore. The car was probably nothing but an embarrassment for the daughter, like the mother. Disappointment wore a body down. He sat for a while thinking about Hattie and finally looking at Stella straight on because her eyes were shut. He could remember the afternoon her father first came into the bar. Harry had been checking bottles, washing glasses, and the afternoon had passed quietly until a voice called out, "You open or closed here or what?"

"Open," Harry answered.

"Didn't see no lights on."

"Light's on back here. Come on back and have a seat."

A man of medium height walked into the shaft of sunlight on the floor. He came up to the counter and said, "It's as dark in here as where I've been all stinking day."

"Sounds like you're working in that salt mine."

"Salt mine's working me. Hell of a stinking job. Anyone else doing any hiring around here? Name's Rafael." He held his hand across the bar and Harry shook it.

"What're you looking for?" Harry asked, noticing the hard muscular body, the stubby nose, the smooth face.

"I'll bust my balls anywhere but inside that stinking hill."

"There's road construction, cabbage picking, a couple of local outfits that build houses. You want something to drink?"

"I don't suppose I came in here for a three-course meal."

"What can I get you?" Harry said evenly. He had learned to keep his comebacks to himself, but from that day on, whenever Rafael came into the bar, he stayed extra quiet and watched. The fight he'd been expecting broke out a few months later when Hattie Doyle refused to leave the bar with him. He called her a snob and shoved her back down in the booth. He did it too hard and her head hit the wall. That was when Harry and a couple of guys went up to him. They walked him outside. When Hattie saw how easily the bum turned soft, she went after him. She couldn't bear to see anyone with their feelings hurt, never mind what they might have done to her. Well, it was her choice. They came in together after that and then she was pregnant and as soon as she had the baby, he got on a road crew that traveled all over the state so he was home only a couple times a month. After a few years of that, he disappeared completely.

When Stella woke up, she put her red dress back on and borrowed his jacket. He took her down to see Buddy at the station, then he took her home. She had to direct him to her house because he had put the circumstances of Hattie Doyle out of his mind so entirely he never even knew where she lived.

It was an ugly place, the porch roof falling in over the summer furniture someone had left out there, the car as big as a boat, floating on its four bald tires in the driveway. He waited on the porch while Stella went in through the front door. She came out a moment later and pulled him inside. He walked through a living room with a worn green rug and a sad-looking sofa to the kitchen, where Hattie sat at the table, washed out and tired looking with a cigarette going in the ashtray beside her. There was an open bag of potato chips in front of her and an open bottle of soda.

"Come on in, Harry!" Her arm seemed independent of her body, which stayed still and flaccid as she waved him inside. "I'm not dressed, but it's a pleasure to see you anyway. Stella, find him a glass. Beer? Soda? What can we get you?"

"I'm fine," Harry said. "Don't trouble yourself."

"No trouble. Cup of coffee? All I have is instant."

"Instant's fine." She seemed bigger and pinker in her bathrobe. With no clothing to hold her in, flesh spilled from her neck down to her belly. She was loose and billowy. Something jiggled every time she moved her hand. Every time she spoke. He glanced at her bosom, trying to read the shapes pressed against the material. Her nipples were as big as saucers.

"Stella, put on the water." Her eyes shot over to his face and caught him. "Now, must be something worth hearing about that brought the two of you walking in my front door together. Your tastes have changed, Harry, if you like them this young."

"Don't insult him," Stella said. "You have no idea what he's done for me."

Hattie picked up her cigarette. "So, isn't this a school day? Why aren't you in school?"

Stella brought two cups of coffee to the table, one for herself, one for Harry. "I did a stupid thing last night. I climbed up to the roof of the building where Smokes and Jokes is and then I couldn't get down. Harry called the firemen and they came and got me and Harry took care of me the whole time I was hanging on the side of the building."

Harry stirred sugar into his coffee and said, "I was up in my kitchen and I saw her across the street."

"Wait a minute," Hattie said. "What do you mean, 'hanging?'"

"Don't ask, mom. I was just being crazy."

"Look, Stella, don't fuck up. Don't give me trouble. You're grounded, you know that? You're going to stay here and study and mind your p's and q's for an entire week. Why would a teacher call for you? Are you in trouble? I wrote her name down by the phone. She called from school just half an hour ago."

Stella went to check by the phone and Hattie turned to Harry and said, "So how's life?"

"She's a great kid and she almost didn't make it. You should be proud of her."

"I am, but she does these crazy things every once in a while and I'm getting tired of it." She gave a phlegmy cough and poured the last of the soda into her glass. "She should think about how things'll end up. If she thought even just a little bit about me, she wouldn't get herself into so much trouble. I wish I knew why that teacher called. It was nine o'clock. She woke me up."

Stella returned, her expression guarded. She looked even thinner and darker next to her mother. Harry realized she knew why the teacher had called but she wasn't going to let on.

Hattie reached into the bag of potato chips and pulled out a handful. "These got less fat in them than eggs and home fries and they're a whole lot easier. That's my breakfast secret. I already had half the bag before you two showed up, but stress makes you eat more. Did you know that, Harry? Here I was thinking she was in school and I come to find out she's been hanging off a building somewheres. So I'm eating. Eating's the way the body comforts itself. I read that. And a person can't deny themselves comfort, know what I mean?

"When you're the only one raising your child and it's a situation where the father don't even send his address, much less any funds, you gotta take comfort. Otherwise I'm a raving maniac. Right, Stella? She's seen me when I get going. She knows. You two had any breakfast?" She flung out her arm. "Stella, the cupboard. Get the big bowl." When Stella set it on the table, Hattie poured out the potato chips and pushed the bowl towards them. "Don't be shy. I got another bag."

Twenty-Seven

When Helene came home from the post office she had a few hours by herself before William would return. The sky over the porch was tinted pink and a rose color hovered in the living room, softening the walls. The couch and chairs looked lumpish and shadowy. A person could study how the different qualities of light coming into a room changed it. Someone who stayed at home every day and had time to notice it. Her mother would have paid attention to the light. She had seemed to understand time and seasons more intimately than anyone else. It was as though she existed on the earth in a way that was closer to the animals.

Uta had moved into the tiny spare room off the living room once Helene and Gunter were old enough to be in the two upstairs bedrooms by themselves. When she died, they had simply closed the door on all of her belongings. And it had remained closed.

Now Helene opened the door and stood inside tentatively. Though all of the surfaces were dusty, the room was as neat as Uta would have kept it. Her mother didn't have many belongings, so the tiny room with only one shelf and a dresser squeezed in next to the small single bed were all she needed to hold her things. The sun, going down over the hillside, glowed in the center of the one window and the room was completely filled by late afternoon light.

Helene sat on the bed and touched the gray blanket that covered it. She had slept in this bed the first few nights after Uta's death just to be close to her mother. Now she felt she was ready to pack up her mother's things. The room was a perfect size for her herbal collection. She could have a table in the center and, for her books and jars, shelves on all the walls.

It was almost pitiful how few things her mother had accumulated. There were only three drawers in the dresser and they held her entire wardrobe. On top of the dresser sat a little box where her mother kept her only jewelry, a pin and a necklace. Had it simply been her nature to be so sparse or was it a habit that grew out of circumstance? Helene tried to remember their apartment in Dresden. She had an impression of carpets and china and walls covered with paintings. One of the few things she remembered distinctly was a little figure under a glass dome that she had spent a lot of time gazing at. The figure was a peddler and on the wagon he pushed there were dozens of miniature things: bowls, yarn, blankets, pots. Every time she looked at it she would find something she hadn't seen before.

Helene went out to the car to get the boxes she had picked up at the supermarket. She had already decided what she would do with Uta's clothes. She would keep the stockings and the socks because they had the same foot size, but the rest of it—the few sweaters and skirts her mother had owned—she would pack up and take to the thrift store.

It went quickly. There were two skirts, three sweaters, three shirts, a small pile of underwear. It all fit in one box. And the clothing was so worn and faded from all the washings, it was hardly worth giving away. Maybe she should simply bury the clothes. Or maybe, better yet, she should take them down to the stream where the joe-pye weed grew and leave them on the banks to disintegrate over the winter. That's what her mother would like her to do; the tall pink flower that bloomed along the stream had been her favorite.

In the bottom drawer she pulled out her mother's hat and scarf and mittens, which smelled faintly of the cedar blocks she kept in the drawer to ward away moths. These she would keep; she'd have what had covered her mother's head and she'd have what had covered her feet. At the bottom of the drawer there was a notebook. She had never seen it before but she knew it wasn't an American variety and must have been something from Germany. All of the pages were filled with her mother's dense small script. She began to read, but it had been a long time since she had read anything in German, so her progress was slow.

Twenty-Eight

~~

Stella waited until her mom left for work before she returned Mrs. Cleveland's call. A woman's warm breathy voice said hello and Stella stammered, "I'm sorry I didn't make it to your class today. I had some problems. Was there something I missed?"

"Not to worry."

Her teacher's voice was so intimate on the phone, she wanted to step away from it.

"Actually, I was calling for another reason. I wondered if we could meet someplace for half an hour so we could talk. Are you free, say, at four-thirty? Can you meet me at the diner?"

She knew it had to do with her speech. Maybe Mrs. Cleveland was going to suggest something to help her mother with her problem. Fine. She'd listen. But she knew Hattie wouldn't be interested. Once she'd signed up for a group called Slender You but after the first meeting, she'd dropped out.

Stella put on her favorite sweater and brushed her hair until it was silky. She dawdled until it was time to leave, not doing much of anything because she couldn't concentrate. She clipped some coupons out of a newspaper, one for a can of beef stew, one for a package of frozen corn, and left them on the table for Hattie to see. Wishful thinking. Anything that wasn't diet or reduced fat was a temptation. If it was there, it would torment her, so when her mother came back from her job at the supermarket, she brought as little food as possible into the house. There was nothing ever that was bulky or filling or nutritious. Hattie only bought food in bags and boxes and bottles. It could be picked and nibbled in small amounts. It didn't go bad and it never had to be cooked or washed.

Stella closed the door behind her and stepped into an afternoon that was cold and gray. She walked through it without leaving a mark on anything. When she opened the door to the restaurant she could see Mrs. Cleveland sitting at a table in the back.

Mrs. Cleveland waved and then gave Stella a big bright greeting. "How are you feeling?"

Stella hung her jacket on the back of her chair and sat down across from her teacher. "I wasn't really sick."

"Oh, I think you already told me that. But I thought it was your time of the month or something."

"No, I'm fine." She knew Mrs. Cleveland was waiting for her to explain why she'd missed school, but, for that moment at least, she decided not to.

"There's something I wanted to talk about. I've been thinking very hard."

Right then the waitress came over. Mrs. Cleveland said, "I

completely forgot about ordering. Here, look at the menu. Whatever you want, it's my treat."

Stella decided to get something not too expensive, so she ordered a tuna fish sandwich and a cup of tea. Mrs. Cleveland got a bowl of soup and a cup of coffee. "The soup here is good," she said. "Why don't you order a bowl too?"

Stella would have liked to, but she shook her head and said just a sandwich was all she could eat.

"Anyway, I've been thinking very hard ever since your speech in class the other day and I guess I really don't know much about your home life, but I got the feeling that maybe it isn't very easy." She paused and looked at Stella. "I wanted to tell you that if you need help with anything, or if you need to talk to someone, I can facilitate that. When things are hard at home sometimes it's helpful just to let somebody know about it. It makes you feel less alone. And when things feel impossible, sometimes the best thing to do is leave for a while and that can be arranged, too. You're never trapped. I want you to understand that."

Stella looked at her blankly. "Where would I go?"

"Well, that's a detail. That's the last step. But if it ever comes to that, things can be arranged. For instance, I have an extra room in my house."

"I don't think I need to leave," Stella said. "But thank you anyway."

"Maybe it would help if we just talked. I'm sure you know that in this world we live in, someone's always telling you how life should be. Movies, TV, magazines. They're always implying that it's a certain way. And if your life doesn't fit their images, sometimes it makes you feel that something's very wrong with you. Of course I'm just repeating the points you made in your speech. But it doesn't apply only to your mother; it can apply to you, too. Your life also doesn't have to be like what you see on TV and in the magazines. Are you close to your mother?"

Stella looked down at her place mat.

"I mean, can you tell your mother about things you're thinking? Do you ever sit down and talk to her?"

Stella folded over the corner of the placemat. "My mother doesn't have it easy. My father left her when I was three years old. She's had to do everything herself and it's been really hard and the last few years she's had this problem with putting on weight. It's an emergency situation so we don't talk about anything else. We can't."

The waitress set their dishes down. Stella noticed the pickles on the plate and the piece of lettuce sticking out from under her bread. Two vegetables. Also, she could see chopped celery mixed in with the tuna fish.

"Emergency?" Faith asked.

"The emergency of getting thin. Nothing else counts. There's this emergency. It's like sirens going off in the house all the time. All attention has to be on this problem."

Faith tried her soup. It was hot and that was all she cared about. "So does it work? Is she able to lose weight?"

"She gets fatter and fatter."

"Does she binge?"

"I don't know what she does. There's no food at home. She lives on soda. It's this big mystery. I'm starving and she's putting on weight."

"Is there anything you can do to help her?"

"Stay out of her way, I guess. Because I can't solve her problem."

"Does she know about your boyfriend and what you're doing at school and stuff like that?"

"She might. I'm not sure."

"What's the hardest thing about being home for you?"

Stella had to think for a minute. It was her life; she'd never tried to ascribe a quality to it. Except to notice that her mother didn't make sense anymore. "I guess it's that most of the time I'm alone. My mom works four to midnight at the supermarket and she sleeps late so I never see her."

"Who does the cooking? Who does the cleaning and the laundry?"

"We don't cook. We're not that kind of a household where you have sit-down meals. We sort of eat out of boxes and bags and I do all the household stuff."

"Do you mind if I ask you how your period is and your health in general?"

"Excuse me?"

"I don't mean to pry, Stella, but do you think you get enough fresh food? Do you have a balanced diet? Do you get your period every month?"

"I used to. I haven't gotten it for the past year."

Faith sighed. She watched Stella bite into her sandwich, saw her thin fingers clutching the bread. "I want you to go see the nurse at school. I think you're undernourished."

"I threw up everything I ate last night. That's why I'm so hungry. I wasn't really sick, it was only nerves."

Faith signaled the waitress and ordered a bowl of soup for Stella. Then she looked into the quiet dark eyes and said,

"When a woman's period stops, it might be stress or it might be that her body isn't getting enough of the right things to eat. If you're not pregnant and your period stopped such a long time ago, something's not right."

"I feel fine," Stella said. The waitress brought the soup. Stella looked at the vegetables floating around in the broth and took the first sip. It had been a long time since she had had soup. Years and years. She had forgotten how comforting it could be.

"I think it's homemade," Faith said. "It's not just out of a can."

Stella's hair swung forward as she leaned down to eat the soup. She threw her hair back out of the way.

"What you said in your speech, about there needing to be a clear-thinking adult in the home, were you talking about your house?"

Stella nodded. "Until she gets thin, there's always the emergency. That's not clear thinking. Nothing else exists except the problem."

There weren't any easy solutions, Faith thought. Good intentions always ran headlong into reality. "It's evident to me that you're not being provided for. You're hungry, your health is being affected, and something needs to be done about it. The best thing might be to take you out of your mother's house for a while and get you on a good wholesome diet. I'll talk to the nurse and she'll take a look at you and then we'll go from there, okay?" She looked at her watch. "Unfortunately, I have another appointment in fifteen minutes so I'm going to have to leave." She stood up and put on her coat. "I hate to run off like this, but let's each think about these possibilities and then let's talk again."

Stella finished the soup, ate the last half of her sandwich, and then she, too, stood up, put on her coat, and walked out of the restaurant into an afternoon that was as damp and gray as before.

Twenty-Nine

*here were some words Helene had to look up in her German dictionary. Also, she read everything out loud. She wanted to hear the sound of the language she hadn't spoken in two years.

At first she thought the notebook was a diary. But when nothing was ever said about feelings on page after page, she began to understand that it was a catalogue of things that had existed before the bombing. Some of the things her mother mentioned she remembered. Some of the people she remembered. She remembered only a few of the places. In one of the entries, she discovered that the peddler who pushed his wagon of odds and ends under the glass dome had been given to her mother by her grandmother, so it was very old.

When she heard William come up the driveway, she took the book into the kitchen. Buster ran up to her and she leaned down to pat his head. "I've been packing up *Mutter's* room."

William was taking off his coat. It was getting dark and he stood in the shadows. "Why are you doing that?"

The question surprised her. There was a sharpness to it, a challenge.

"Isn't it time?"

"Actually, I liked having her there."

"I did, too, but I needed some place for all of my herbs." She felt defensive suddenly because she realized she had never thought of asking William and it was, after all, his house. But she paid half of the expenses and she had assumed it was also her house. "I hope you don't mind."

"I'm going to miss having that little piece of her."

"So will I," Helene said and she knew she would. "But I saved her hat and her scarf and her mittens and I have her boots and her shoes."

"Her scarf is something I'd like to have, Helene, if you don't mind."

"Of course. I'm sorry, William, I should have asked you. There was something else I found in there. It's in German and I've been reading it." She held the book out to him. He sat down at the table to look at it but it was too dark to see. Helene switched on the light and in the sudden clarity she understood that there was a competitiveness between them over Uta's belongings. Why wasn't it clear to him that her claim was greater? William had been a friend, a deep, close friend, but a friend only. Over his shoulder she started to read. First she read in German and then slowly she translated.

"*Wolff is walking up the sidewalk towards me. The bells in the cathedral are ringing. Children's voices call out in the park. I hear the splash of water in the fountain. He is smiling. He* *seems to—*I guess it's own—*to own the world as he comes towards me. It is springtime. The streets smell of the blossoming trees. Have you seen the ducklings in the park? he asks me. There is such pleasure in his handsome face.*"

"Who was Wolff?" William asked.

"I guess he was a boyfriend of hers." Helene paused. "He could have been my father. The next piece is also about him."

The last time I saw Wolff he wore his uniform. I made him take it off as soon as he came inside and leave it on the floor. I will not have that uniform in my apartment. So he visited me wearing his undergarments. I told him what had happened to the Singers downstairs. He said most likely they were at Theresienstadt and that it was a very well-run place, a model ghetto, and I shouldn't worry.

The night before they were taken away, Frau Singer played so late I fell asleep to her music.

It was always cooler down by the river. There were restaurants where you could order refreshing drinks and choose from a tray of sweets. Musicians played on the Brülsche Terrasse. At night, the boats carried lanterns. They were green and red. Someone would often be singing.

They stopped long enough to have dinner. After dinner, she read more to him. "I want to hear the whole book," William said. It was getting late and she was tired. He saw her look at the clock. "Not all of it right now, of course, but little by little. It's incredible. Do you realize how incredible it is? If you wrote a translation of it, Helene, we could have it published."

"But it's just her memories. I don't think anyone else would find it interesting."

"Don't you see? She's recreated a place and a time that was wiped out. Ultimately, this book is a testament to the indefatigability of the human mind. We erased that city and all of those people, but here it is. It still exists."

"But it's something private. Listen." Helene read the next piece in German, then, because she was tired, she had to study it a while before she could figure it out in English.

"*In the winter, Hannah's cheeks turn bright red. When she comes in, she brings the smell of cold. She wears long skirts and heavy socks and often has an apple in her smock. Her eyes are blue and they glitter when it gets cold. We talk about boyfriends. Always boyfriends. Hannah pays no attention to policy. No, maybe that's politics. We talk about the old men we took care of in the hospital, how they tried to get close with us.*"

"She worked in a hospital?"

"She was a nurse."

"She never told me that."

"It's in here. There's lots about the hospital and the people in the hospital. She never told you that she was a nurse and she never told me about my father. I think the reason is that it was all gone. That's why it's in this book. And it's in the book so that she didn't have to live it anymore."

"But she should have told you about your father."

"She should have. But she couldn't."

Thirty

◦◦◦

*I*n the winter, Uta wound scarves around her neck. Not even
scarves, but pieces of cotton she'd cut from dresses Helene
no longer wore, or shirts of William's that she had decided
were worn past mending. She wound them around her neck
for warmth, and with her hair spilling out of her hairpins and
her rough red cheeks she was a picture. He should have pulled
a chair over to her and gotten up on it to kiss her.

One year she raised turkeys. Three were eaten by raccoons
and the other seven grew to full size. At Thanksgiving she said
they were too small for butchering, but at Christmas they
butchered all but two. Those two lived with them for five
years, pecking at the windows for her when she was in the
house, running up whenever she came out the door. If it was
warm and sunny, the tom paraded with his feathers open. His
head would turn colors, changing from red to blue as he

courted the hen. Maybe he was courting Uta, too. William saw her go out with a bucket of corn and call, "Goodnik! Goodnik!" Even if the turkeys were grazing behind the chicken house they came running. She'd throw the corn out and watch as they stood on their long slender legs and picked it up in their beaks. He could see her standing there, a short stocky woman with rubber boots on her feet, scarves around her neck, a long skirt and an old hunting jacket she'd found somewhere. She always wore cast-offs. He also saw her in the kitchen plucking the pinfeathers from a dead bird, working till she got every single one, no matter how long it took her.

How silly for a life like that to end only a quarter of a mile from the house in such an ordinary, stupid way. Surely, a woman who had witnessed the bombing of that incredible city, who had walked into another country with a small child, who had come close to starving, a woman who had traveled to a place where she knew no one and didn't speak the language, surely someone as brave and heroic as that deserved death in a bedroom at an old age, surrounded by the people who cared about her. And didn't he, after all, deserve to have her longer?

William knew there was no such thing as fairness, but didn't the happiness of a man who had been insulted and ridiculed all of his life mean anything?

It did not. Of course it did not. He was as stupid as Eloise Baldwin if he thought there was such a thing as equal treatment. He got down off his chair and moved the ladder over to the Oddities section. He had shelved her book on the top because he wanted to keep it around a while longer. He opened to the section on death and read the first poem he came to:

Doves cooing in the barn
Crickets singing o'er the farm
Can death bring its harm
To a valley so green, so sweet?

By now she must have answered her own question, which was the same one that he, a more educated thinker, nevertheless asked as well. He would put it differently, of course, but it was still the basic and arrogant query: Why here? Why her? Why me?

Buster lifted his head as Faith walked up to the front door. William put the book back and climbed down the ladder.

"Is dinner still on for tonight?" Faith asked. "I'm looking forward to it. Is there anything I can bring? A bottle of wine, an hors d'oeuvre?"

"Helene has it all planned," William said, climbing off the ladder, "so come empty-handed."

"Nothing at all? Where does Helene find all that time to cook?"

"She does it in the mornings before she goes to work. I always sleep late, but I hear her puttering around."

"A truly organized woman."

"She likes to cook. She's a wonderful cook. She learned it from her mother. Tea? The water's hot."

"Oh yes, thank you." Faith sat down on the rocker. "It's been a grueling day. But I can't stay long because I have to go home and get ready."

William didn't have to ask what kind of tea she wanted or whether she took it with lemon. When he thought about it, he really knew quite a lot about her. More than tea preferences, of course. That she lived alone. That she was careful and kind. That she worried a lot.

"You know what I realized today?" Her eyes followed him as he walked to his desk. "Our educational system is lacking something really essential. Maybe it's the availability of television and movies, I don't know. But it seems to me that I spend half my time being a counselor to these kids because somewhere they got the notion that everything should be easy and so at the first difficulty, they fall apart. Or else it's the other extreme. They have the notion that it's all supposed to be hard and they don't deserve a chance to have it any better. It's one thing or the other, black or white. They miss all that in-between stuff, the little victories, the little setbacks. They don't see them. I do really think it's a symptom of a culture that doesn't read literature anymore. If they read books, my God, they would know that life is full of variation."

"Not all books," William said

"Come on, novels and poetry set out to examine the differences, the complexities. That's their purpose. You're the last person I'd expect to argue with that."

"I'm not arguing. You're right. I was just being facetious because recently a book of very bad poems by a deceased local poet came into my hands and I've been marveling over how simpleminded the writing is."

"Oh really? Who is it by?"

"I shouldn't have even brought it up," William said. "I don't feel like climbing the ladder to get it down again, but I'll bring it home tonight and you'll see what I mean."

"It's frustrating," Faith said, returning to her earlier asser-
tion. "Kids today don't have any sense of the challenge!"

"Inspire them. Have them read Shakespeare and show
them all the layers. Let them hear the music and the lament
and the praise."

"Yes, yes, I know. More than anyone, an English teacher
really has the chance to wake them up."

"You can do it."

"Sometimes I can. But sometimes I can't." She looked at her
watch. "Listen, is this a fancy affair or is it blue jeans?"

"Fancy? At my house? Come in your pajamas if you feel
like it."

William watched Faith walk to the door and thought again
of Uta. She had been looser down at the hips than this woman.
This woman was a scholar and his Uta had been a peasant.
Only a peasant, a person not afraid of the unknown, would
take his hand and walk with him back to his bedroom.

Thirty-One

*H*elene had another hour at the post office before she could go home and work on dinner. There would be four altogether—Harry, William, Faith, and herself. She didn't know Faith. She lived in a housing development near the highway so she wasn't in and out the way the locals were.

She thought about what she would serve as she sorted mail. She wanted a dinner with symmetry. From the chicken soup to the apple pie, she wanted a balance of tastes and textures. Except that pie wasn't right, it was too doughy. How about a pudding, only mildly sweet. That was it. Butterscotch pudding. It was a Hugel family tradition. There was often pudding on the stove in Dresden and when her mother had been alive there was often pudding on the stove at William's. It was a dessert Americans didn't understand. For Helene, the challenge was to get it smooth and soft, but firm. Also, it had to be served cool. A firm smooth pudding was proof that the solid and liquid could find a place of perfect suspension within a pleasing temperature. It testified to the fact that opposites belonged together. She had read once that in the days when everyone traveled by horseback, women often carried pudding in a burlap sack that hung from the saddle, the horses' movements keeping it well-mixed.

Harry had probably never had a bowl of pudding in his life. For that matter, had he ever slept in a small unheated bedroom at the top of a farmhouse? Anyplace a body could sleep, Harry most likely had been there.

Of course, he might not sleep with her ever again. She might end it with him when she walked him out to his car after dinner. It all depended. If he could tell them a story, she'd let him stay.

Thirty-Two

~~~

When William opened the back door, he saw snow. The valley was still; the flakes coming down were large and feathery. It was only October eighth but the snow was covering the road quickly. He whistled for Buster, his breath curling in front of him like smoke. Beyond the circle of light, he saw a mysterious shape in the darkness. It was the dog standing over some kind of dead animal. A deer. A very small one, maybe a fawn. Buster had probably found it in the woods and dragged it over to the back door to show it off. The eyes were gone but the rest of it looked untouched. The hooves were black and pointed, dainty. Helene came to the door. "Look what Buster found," he said.

"I know you think it's a fine idea, Buster, but our dinner guests aren't going to like it. Can we drag it off?"

"He'll find the scent wherever we take it. I'll have to drive it away."

"Be quick. They'll be coming soon."

When William came out again with his jacket, the dog looked at him expectantly. "Not this time. The mighty carrion eater is staying home."

He dragged the frozen carcass over to his truck, pulled and pushed till he got it up onto the tailgate, and then shoved it onto the bed. "So what happened to you?" he asked the soft human-looking face. Snowflakes glistened on the fur. "Hunting season hasn't even started. Who brought you down, coyotes? Are they the ones that got your eyeballs?" He walked around to the driver's side and climbed into the seat. When he turned onto the road, the snow was coming down hard, flying into the windshield diagonally. He switched his high beams to low and the snow jumped back.

He could have pulled over anywhere and pushed the body out, but the snow was so beautiful he drove on a bit farther and turned up a dirt road. At the top of the hill he stopped the truck. With his headlights off, the darkness was total and the falling snow was the only sign that something else besides him was alive and breathing. He went to the back of the truck and opened the gate. Instead of pulling her out by her legs, he put his arms underneath the fawn and gently lifted. But leaning in to get a better purchase, he caught the odor he had missed somehow when he had been handling her before, and in the weak light shining out from the cab, saw white strings moving on her chest. Maggots. He jumped back. She was crawling with them. He seized her hooves and pulled her down onto the snow. There. The snow would hold her until other animals came along and finished her off.

When he got back into the cab, he imagined maggots

crawling up his arm. He could feel them inching under his shirt, slipping under his collar. He started the motor, turned on the light to high beams, and drove down the hill fast, the snow speeding right into his eyes.

How could he have been so deluded? Her body, which he could still touch with his hands, which he could still see in the yard feeding the chickens and in the kitchen standing over the stove, had surrendered, in the same way the deer had, to nature's anonymous cycle. She was covered with maggots, too. They had eaten her flesh entirely. He pictured her skeleton, the empty sockets of her eyes, the bits of hair sticking to her skull.

Thirty-Three

F aith stepped out of the shower. She wiped the fog off the mirror with her towel and gave herself a satisfied glance. Her body was firm, her thighs tight, and everything fit together like a form patted into shape with thoughtful hands. If Lucille had been there, she'd have combed out Faith's wet hair. She'd have coaxed it behind Faith's ears to make her look butch and if they didn't have anyplace to go, Faith would have let her rub gel into it so the curls would disappear. Lucille would button a black vest over Faith's naked chest. She'd kneel down at Faith's feet and have her step into a pair of skintight black leather pants, which she'd pull up over Faith's bare backside. It made Faith feel transformed. They would go somewhere else in the apartment, say, out to the kitchen to make a meal, and in the process, they'd fall down onto the couch together and Lucille would undress her with the same slow attention.

When Lucille got out of the shower, Faith never tried to put her into a costume. Her friend couldn't be any other way than she was. From the time she was eleven, she had known she would never be physical with a man. They just weren't interesting. Faith, on the other hand, had boyfriends through college and didn't discover until many years afterwards why she'd always found sex disappointing. She'd been sleeping with the wrong gender. It was that simple. A man you could never dress up, you could never talk to at three A.M., you could never tell secrets to. They didn't reveal their fantasies. They didn't ask you to describe your idea of a perfect evening. They didn't give you sponge baths and lick your fingers and toes. They didn't go with you to ten stores to find exactly the right bedspread. Lucille did all of those things. Even more.

Faith looked at her face in the mirror. She ran her fingers across her wide forehead, over her hollow cheeks and very softly around her lips. She stroked her neck. She closed her eyes and laid her hands over the lids, feeling the shape of her eyeballs. She repeated to herself the things Lucille had told her. "You are so lovely. You are so beautiful and I love you so much. My beauty. My beauty." She squirted a bit of gel into her hands and rubbed it into her short hair. Then she combed her curls back flat against her head the way Lucille did. The face in the mirror looked stark and mannish. It also looked doubtful. She put her hands back on her cheeks and, stroking up and down, said, "I'm with you, lovely woman, we're in this together."

Thirty-Four

A s soon as Stella walked into the drugstore, she knew she wasn't there to steal anything. What she wanted was information, clues, hints, suggestions. She felt overwhelmed. Since her meeting with Mrs. Cleveland, the darkness she always knew was in her body had risen so high she could feel it in her throat. She kept on swallowing to try to push it down.

The drugstore was empty. Her sneakers made a soft padding sound as she walked from aisle to aisle, looking for something. At the magazine rack, she picked up *Time* and leafed through it, stopping to look at the people in the ads and read the headlines under the biggest pictures. There was a story about the stock market with a photograph of men in gray suits walking across a huge floor. Just the size of the room suggested their power. There was another story about Vietnamese pigs that people were keeping as pets. They were as intelligent and friendly as dogs. She picked up *People* magazine and looked at the clothes the women were wearing. Short skirts, scooped necks, slacks that didn't hide anything. They all looked tanned and happy, even the ones who were getting divorced. Then she picked up *Glamour*. The first page she turned to had *fat* in the title. *Fat Slides Off With Acupuncture*. The article took up the entire page and next to it, there was a bright glossy picture of a woman her mother's size with needles in her ear. Stella swallowed. Then she read the article through twice in case she had missed anything. She thought it should say more, like how much it cost, whether you had to live in Chicago where they did it, and also the great things that happened to the people afterwards. But it only talked about how the clinic got started and gave an explanation of how the acupuncture worked. At the bottom of the page there was an address and a phone number. She dug around in her knapsack, found a pen, and wrote the information on the palm of her hand. Maybe that was the answer she was looking for.

When she went outside, a light feathery first snow of the winter was falling. It was kindness coming out of the sky. She put her head back and the wet dreamy flakes landed on her upturned face. The snow was whiter than white, glistening, silent. The flakes were enormous and they covered the grimy village quickly. Her mother would be cursing. She had skidded down last winter's snowy streets and said she was going to save up to buy snow tires for this year, but Stella didn't think she'd done it yet. She had probably convinced herself that summer was going to last forever.

The car was gone when Stella walked down the driveway and because there weren't any tracks, she knew Hattie had left before the snow. Inside, the house was cold. To save money, they turned the furnace down whenever they weren't home. Once, the pipes had frozen up that way, but after they were thawed, the man had wrapped them in heat tape. It was unlikely to happen again, but on really cold nights, before she went to bed, Stella would leave the water trickling. Of course, Hattie would turn it off when she came home sometime later, denying reality, having decided that she wasn't the kind of woman who would buy a house with pipes that ran along the exterior wall.

The ashtray on the kitchen table was full of cigarette stumps and there were three empty soda cans next to the sink. But the dishes were done and there was a box containing a frozen pot-pie on the counter with an orange sticker on it because it had been marked down. A present from her mother. She wondered if there was any new food since she'd looked in the refrigerator that morning, but it contained the same three items: cottage cheese, saltines, and soda.

At the table she opened her hand to look at the phone number. There was a dominance of sevens, which matched the pattern of her own phone number. She took it as more than coincidence, as proof that this kitchen was the place she was supposed to live in, gray and dirty as it might be. She glanced up and saw the perfect organization of it, how the table in the center was just the right size and how the worn countertop and faded linoleum had a soft brown quality that toned out the glare of the fluorescent light on the ceiling. They'd repaired the torn seat on one of the chairs with duct tape and the gray strip across the red plastic with the snow outside the window behind it made her feel resigned and sad.

"Some situations you are better off just leaving," Mrs.

Cleveland had said. But this tiny kitchen at the back of the house, sagging into its rotten foundation, was the place she was meant to stay. She held the phone up to her ear and dialed. It didn't go through. Then she remembered that with long distance you had to dial a one before the area code and so with more confidence she tried it a second time. As she waited for someone to answer, she thought about the chicken potpie she would have in entirety, thanks to her mother. A warm buttery dinner on the first snowy night of the year was also a good sign.

"Olive Johnstone Clinic," a voice said.

"Hi," she stammered. "Um, can anybody go to this place? I mean, do you have to live in Chicago?"

"Just a moment, please." Stella was put on hold. The Muzak was playing "Autumn Leaves." She held the phone clapped to her ear because she was afraid of losing the connection. Outside the window, snow was spilling over the garbage can lid, which someone had forgotten to put on top of the garbage can. The snow covered a jug of antifreeze that had been lying around since last winter and blurred the shed, which many years ago had housed someone's chickens and now held only garbage.

"Yes, may I help you?"

"Can I have some information? Like, is this place only for people who live in Chicago? I mean, if they want to lose weight? I read about it in New York State and I was wondering about it for my mother."

"Are you referring to the acupuncture clinic?"

"Oh, yes, sorry."

"Hold, please, while I transfer you to the annex."

When the second female voice said, "Hello, Olive Johnstone Clinic, The Annex," Stella was ready with her question.

"My mother lives in New York State and I was wondering if she could come to the clinic and how much it costs."

"Yes, for people who live out of state there is a registration fee, but with all the publicity we've been getting, slots are disappearing fast, so if you can give me your address, I'd be happy to mail you a form, which you would return with the fee."

"How much is that, please?"

"The registration fee is twenty-five dollars."

"Is that the only fee?"

"That's the only fee the clinic charges."

"Does she live at this place or where does she stay and how long does it take?"

"All treatment is performed on an out-patient basis only, so she would have to find accommodations. Most of our patients enroll in the program for two weeks. Each day's session runs from nine to three."

"Well, thanks. Oh, one other thing, where are you located?"

"We're at 1900 West Polk Street, Cook County Hospital, west of the Loop. Any further questions?"

"No," Stella said. "Thank you."

She assumed they would find it easily enough with a map. Since Chicago was on a lake it would be warmer, and if they took blankets and pillows, they could just park at the hospital and sleep in the car. She'd get Hattie to the front door by nine o'clock and then hang out at a library or museum until three o'clock, when she'd go back to pick her up. Why, she could learn a foreign language in two weeks of six-hour days in the library, or she could study art history at the museum and come back knowing all kinds of things she hadn't known before, and she and Darryl could have long intellectual conversations.

She could take buses to the important buildings and learn about Chicago's history. She could write her term paper. She could study for the history exam. Why, she could probably accomplish more in two weeks working on her own than she could in two weeks going to school.

She put her dinner in the oven and went upstairs to get her boots from last year. Darryl would just be getting out of basketball practice. If she ran, she could catch him before he started home.

It was amazing how the world changed once a person had a purpose. The railroad bridge against the hill was black and definite; the trees below it stood out against the sky. The snow had disguised the trash in the yards, and scumbled the edges of the houses so that everything that was leaning and broken apart looked whole. Passing a rusted, doorless car sunken onto collapsed tires, she decided she liked this part of town. Growing up in this neighborhood forced a person to rely on herself. Kids who lived here weren't spoiled. They were simply left alone to figure stuff out for themselves.

The windows in the high school looked black and the snow that sat along the ledges made a series of white lines. It was as if a huge piece of black-and-white fabric hung against the sky and since it was her lucky day and all the elements were slipping into the pattern, she could see a red block of color moving along the bottom. She waved her arms and called. Darryl, in his bright red jacket, stepped out of the crowd of guys he was walking with and shouted, "Hey, Stel, where you going?"

"I came to find you," she said when she reached him. She took his arm and walked him in the other direction. She wanted to tell him how suddenly she knew where she belonged and what she had to do and that she had discovered beauty in ordinary things. She wanted to show him the inside of her palm, which contained the answer to everything. Instead, she took him to the drugstore and gave him the article to read.

"Wow, acupuncture! Are you going to call them?"

"I have. We're going. We're going to leave tomorrow. We have to stay up there for two weeks. It's going to take about five hundred bucks."

"How are you going to get five hundred bucks by tomorrow?"

"Maybe from you is what I was hoping." She said it straight out, fast. Then she added, "Like a loan."

She saw a pulsing in his jaw as he put the magazine back on the rack. "You think I'm Mr. Moneybags or something? Where am I going to get five hundred dollars?"

"Please."

"Please what? I don't have it."

The woman who worked at the restaurant was standing behind them, waiting for them to move out of the way so she could get a newspaper. Darryl caught Stella's arm and pulled her into the next aisle. She whispered, "Couldn't you forge your mother's name on a check? She wouldn't even notice." She was thinking of the way Darryl's mother was always telling her dinner guests how it had cost her an extra twenty thousand dollars to save the tree in their backyard. Wasn't her son's girlfriend's mother worth just a fraction of that? Surely, she wouldn't miss a measly five hundred.

"You don't know her. She's a hawk. She'd spot it in a minute. Look..." He pulled her back against a display of shampoo. "I really want to help. You know I do, but I'm not going to rip off my parents. Think of something else."

"Let's get out of here, okay?"

They walked back to the school and over to her side of town, sliding through soft, slippery snow. Now the bridge had melted into the sky and the trees that had seemed so stark and lonely before were invisible. She expected to smell dinner as soon as she opened the door, and when she didn't, she remembered that her mother had never replaced the element in the oven when it had stopped working. "Thirty dollars!" Hattie had said in disgust after she'd called the repairman. "We never use the goddamn thing anyway."

"She needs to get better," Stella said, sitting down on the patched chair. "I've got to find five hundred dollars. Food and gas and maybe a couple of nights in a motel in Chicago, maybe four hundred's all I need."

"There's a pawn shop in Sharon. Can you sell anything?"

"The TV's ancient. We don't have a radio. What could I sell?"

They both looked at the refrigerator at the same time. "Think I'd get four hundred dollars?"

"Probably not, maybe two hundred. Anything else around?"

The toaster was a piece of junk. They didn't have a microwave. That left the stove. No one would have to know the oven didn't work. "Okay," she said, "but how would we get them out of here?"

"Drive to Chicago on Sunday. I'll borrow my uncle's truck and I'll get a couple of guys and we'll be here early tomorrow morning."

"We can't. She'll be hungover. She doesn't work on

Saturday so she always goes to Harry's on Saturday night."

"Okay, we'll load tonight, drive to the pawnshop early tomorrow morning and you can leave for Chicago in the afternoon."

"I don't know. I think Chicago's pretty far away. How does it work anyway? When you take things to a pawn shop, you get them back, right?"

"I think so. Nobody's going to buy this stuff, it's too beat up. So don't worry, I'm sure it will still be there."

"You're sure? You think I should do it?"

"Sell this shit?" Darryl asked. "I think you ought to try."

"I could clean them and shine them so they looked really good. You think you can get the truck?"

"Maybe."

"What are you going to tell him it's for?"

"I'm going to say it's to move my girlfriend's mother's furniture."

Suddenly she felt as though everything was going to work out.

"Listen, I have to get going. The hawk wants me home at six o'clock sharp. I'll call my uncle and if it's a go, we can load the stuff up this evening.

As soon as he was out the door, she filled a saucepan with water, set the potpie inside it, and put it on a burner to steam. Goddamn it, she was going to have potpie for dinner.

Thirty-Five

~~~

A ll the preparations were finished. The food was staying warm in the oven, hors d'oeuvres were on the table, candles were lit. Harry was the first to arrive. His cigarette odor was covered with the smell of cold air so that when Helene kissed him hello, she felt as though she were kissing the night itself. He set a six-pack of imported German beer on the table. "Was I supposed to bring anything else?"

"Just you," she said.

"So these are the digs!" He poked his head into the living room and looked around. "What do you and your uncle do, split expenses?"

"Pretty much."

"And you have a bedroom over the kitchen and he has a bedroom downstairs someplace?"

"We're at opposite ends of the house."

"And you spend a lot of time in here, in the kitchen?"

"I like to cook. My mother showed me. She also showed me a lot about healing herbs, which was something her mother passed on to her. She started this herb collection I've been trying to keep going." Helene pointed to shelves with neatly labeled jars holding leaves and roots and stems. "Every year I try to get out to replace what's in these with fresh. See the dates? I'm fixing up a room to move all of this stuff into so I can expand. There's so much out there. I want to learn as much as I can."

"You don't use medicine?"

"Drugstore medicine? I never have. Some of these cure spirit problems and there isn't a medicine for that anyway." She took down a jar that contained leaves. "This helps sadness. You make a tea from it."

"So what's the magic herb?"

"It's vervain. It stands very tall and it only has one blossom on each of its spikes so it makes great beauty with only a few flowers."

"You're not telling me that a flower can cure sadness?"

"Sure I am. Just as this"—she took out another jar—"makes men more virile."

He could see flat yellowish leaves.

"That's one you don't need, but maybe this one..." She showed him a jar full of roots. "This relaxes you."

"So where'd you get all this stuff?"

"It's from the fields and hills, right around here. I hardly ever go off the property."

"You got one for indigestion? I always get this gas after I eat." He took her hand and put it on his stomach. "I can always feel it here."

"A digestive aid, that's what you want. I'll make you a tea."
As she put the kettle on the stove she saw headlights coming
up the driveway. It wasn't William because they were smaller
headlights than those on the truck, close to the ground. Buster,
who was usually calm with visitors, started to bark. When
Helene went to open the door, she saw Faith huddled under
the outside lamp, looking small and pale. "Come in, come in!"
she called, flinging open the door and throwing the warmth of
the kitchen onto the snow.

"I wasn't sure if this was the right place. All the landmarks
William gave me were so hazy with this storm I had to guess
at every turn."

"I know. It took us all by surprise, didn't it? But it's beautiful, yes?" Buster barked again and Helene said, "Quiet, mister,
she's a friend."

"I don't know if I would call it beautiful. The roads are
really getting covered."

"Well, don't worry. I'm sure it won't be snowing by the
time you're ready to leave. It's supposed to be flurries, no real
accumulation. May I take your coat?"

Faith came inside.

"William's on a last-minute errand," Helene said. "But he'll
be home soon." As she carried the other woman's jacket to the
closet, she noticed the softness of the leather and the expensive
weight and feel it had.

Harry came out of the living room and held out his hand. "I
thought I had met everyone in town here, but I guess that's a
lot of bullshit because I don't think I've had the pleasure. I'm
Harry. I own Better Days on Main Street." When he grasped
her hand, he was shocked at how small and cold it was.

Helene put crackers and cheese on the table and poured Faith a glass of wine. They moved into the living room.

"Helene told me you teach at the high school," Harry said.

"I teach ninth-and eleventh-grade English."

She didn't smile when she looked at him and the way she sat in the chair, legs crossed, arms crossed, a world unto herself, he knew how she felt about men. It didn't kill his interest, though; a woman with a sharp, hard exterior like that was a challenge. "That's the age when there's only one thing on their minds," he said, "and believe me it ain't English."

"Actually..." She uncrossed her legs and opened her hands on her lap. "We have a very exciting curriculum. School's changed since you went there, Harry. They read and write and talk about relevant issues. It's very issue-oriented. We find it keeps their interest."

"No more Shakespeare?"

"We even work Shakespeare into it."

"I remember we had to memorize these..." Harry looked thoughtful. "Well, poems I guess they were. But there was a special word for them, by some English poet, and we'd have to recite them in front of the class. Once a week. It was torture."

"Maybe it was sonnets? By Keats, perhaps?"

"Hell if I remember."

"We give our students Keats. There's one that goes like this." Faith's voice changed. It seemed bigger than Harry would have thought it could be, and the words came out sweetly like they were a song.

When I have fears that I may cease to be
  Before my pen has gleaned my teeming brain,

Before high-piléd books, in charact'ry,
    Hold like rich garners the full-ripened grain;
When I behold, upon the night's starred face,
    Huge cloudy symbols of a high romance,
And think that I may never live to trace
    Their shadows, with the magic hand of chance;
And when I feel, fair creature of an hour,
    That I shall never look upon thee more,
Never have relish in the faery power
    Of unreflecting love;—then on the shore
Of the wide world I stand alone, and think,
Till Love and Fame to nothingness do sink.

"Yeah! That's it! 'When I have fears that I may cease to be.' I remember that line. I remember it! Oh God, Helene!"

"What?" She was in the kitchen.

"I just heard a poem I used to know when I was fifteen."

"It's been stored in your memory all those years," Faith said.

"Yeah, that and Erik Rotweiler. He sat behind me so he always went after I did. He could never get those things out of his mouth whole and the teacher, who was truly a sadistic bitch, wouldn't let him sit down until he had stumbled over every goddamned word. The agony, I'll never forget it."

"That's another thing that's changed. We don't shame students anymore. We don't ask them to do something in front of other people that they clearly can't do. That shame stays with them for the rest of their lives and to be the one responsible for creating it...well, that's not what I want to be remembered for."

"We were all just sitting there dying for that kid. I'm telling you, it was excruciating."

"Well, there are still difficult moments in classrooms, times when other kids are just holding their breath for the kid at the front, but it's over something entirely different. It's sharing, comradeship, understanding; it's certainly not suffering someone else's shame."

They heard a car door slam outside. The door to the house was thrown open and William came into the kitchen. He stood there, looking at them. Then he started speaking in a flat, level voice: "The dead have no affection for what they were. No affection. They go back to zero. Once they leave us, they're in a hurry to throw it all off and get back to the most basic elements they contain. I never knew that. Excuse me."

He went down a hallway and disappeared. It was quiet until Helene said, "Well, that was a dramatic entrance. Can I get you more wine, Faith?"

"No, I'm fine. With this storm, I don't want to drink too much of this stuff." She touched her hair absentmindedly. Then she remembered. It was stiff and flat. She brushed her cheek with her fingertips. "To get back to what I was saying, I'll give you an example of the kind of sharing I was referring to."

Harry could see that when a lady didn't like sex, her passion went into other things.

"I assigned my eleventh-grade students a five-minute position speech on any controversial issue they were interested in and one young woman decided to talk about the pressure in our culture to look a certain way. The point she wanted to make was that our culture preaches only one image, it doesn't preach variety. For people who want to fit that image but can't, it haunts them."

"Like how?" Harry asked.

"Take, for instance, someone who wants to be thin but can't. The perpetual dieter."

"Oh yeah, I know someone like that." Harry leaned forward in his chair as though it would help him to focus on what he was going to tell her, but really, it was only to get a better perspective on Faith's body. She had a pert chest even though she was a tight woman. "I got a customer, she's not an alcoholic, but she's a drinker. Believe me, there's a difference. She comes in every Saturday night, that's the only time I see her. I've known her for years. Back when she was young and pretty I knew her. But somewheres along the line she turned enormous. She eats to make up for what life didn't give her. And you can tell she hates what she's become, still wishes she was that thin little girl."

"Yes, I imagine so. You must see a lot of misfortune in the people who come to your place."

Helene came in, wiping her hands on a dish towel. "Harry has a lot of stories. Getting him to tell them is another matter."

"I'm not the storyteller, I'm the bartender. But it's simple. In a nutshell, what I've seen is ordinary life—your run-of-the-mill ordinary life—but taken to all its extremes: lust, rage, and pure craziness. Craziness is what this woman is. It looks like she's sitting there right in front of you, she certainly takes up enough space, but when she starts to talk, you realize nothing makes sense. The planet of common sense we all live on? She's slipped off it."

Helene turned to him. "Ordinary life doesn't have to be taken to its extremes to be interesting. Sometimes simple mysteries are more provocative."

"And this woman's extreme, I tell you. Helene, can I have a beer now that I've finished my tea?"

"Certainly!" As she opened the fridge, she called out to Harry, "Just leave room for food. We're eating three courses, from soup to pudding."

"I'm with you all the way," Harry proclaimed. He took a sip from his bottle and said, "Helene can cure depression. I'm not depressed but I do have indigestion and Helene can cure that, too."

"I can't cure depression, Harry, don't exaggerate. It's tea made from vervain. What I can do is pay attention and notice mysteries."

"What do you mean, 'notice mysteries'?" Faith asked.

"What I like is the world in its ordinary state. I don't like going to bars because everything there is so extreme. I think the alcohol makes it that way. Harry and I, the other day, noticed a window open in the Baldwin Mercantile Building on Main Street. There were two kids up there in a room that's usually vacant and so we've been thinking about it and doing a little investigating and trying to put two and two together to see what we can come up with."

"Helene, something happened."

"See, and Harry keeps his eye on it and then he tells me what he sees and, I don't know, it's just interesting. My mother, you see, she was a short woman but she had great experience. There was so much in her memory. Living through the bombing of Dresden, coming here after the war when she knew no one, putting a life together with Uncle William. I have great respect for her. After the bombing, she had nothing. Literally nothing except for the memory of that horrible experience. But there was something inside her that let her move forward. She followed hints, clues, and eventually they led her to this. Since she's been gone, everything around me has seemed flat. I had to find a mystery somewhere and I think maybe I did. So what else happened, Harry?"

Harry put his bottle on the floor and leaned back in the chair with his hands behind his head in a posture that looked like total relaxation. But as soon as he started talking he came forward again. He couldn't pose when he talked about Stella; he had to tell it straight. "The girl came back the next night. She climbed out the window and danced up on the rooftop. Then she almost fell climbing back down and luckily, I happened to see her so I called the fire company. I'll tell you, it was a damn close call."

"When did this happen?"

"A few days ago. I'm sorry, Helene, I should have told you about it right away."

"Did you talk to her?"

"Talk to her? Hell, I drove her home and we told her mother what had happened."

"Who is this girl?" Faith asked.

William came into the living room with Buster behind him. His hair was wet and his face was red and shiny. He'd changed his clothes but it looked like he'd taken a shower, too. "I might have one of those beers, Harry. Are they in the fridge?"

"Did you get rid of it?" Helene asked.

"I took it up Baldwin Road. It was slow going. The snow on the hilltop was fierce."

"But you dumped it?"

"I dumped it. What she's talking about," William said to Faith and Harry, "is a deer carcass that Buster dragged home this evening and which I had to transport off the property far enough away so he wouldn't find it again. I took it to the top of Baldwin Road and when I was lifting it out of the truck I saw that it was infested with maggots. Thousands of them. They were crawling all over it and on me."

"At this time of year, maggots? How come they weren't killed by the frost?" Helene could sense another mystery.

"That's a good question," William answered. "Maybe maggots are alive in the winter."

"How could they be?" Helene asked.

"Maybe the deer was in a protected place. Maybe Buster dragged it out of an old shed."

"Yes, but it freezes in old sheds," Helene said. "How could those maggots still be alive?"

"They weren't alive when I first put the deer in the truck. Maybe that's it, they weren't alive at first, but then maybe the bed of the truck got a little warm and maybe they had never been frozen all the way through. So it didn't take long.

"I had the heat on full blast and maybe it was warming the back of the truck, too, so they defrosted and went into action. The deer, which seemed perfectly odorless when I stuck it in, had a smell when I took it out and I guess that was because of the heat as well. But it made me understand something. I had a realization up there on Baldwin Hill." He looked at Faith because this was the kind of thing they liked to talk about in the store. "Nothing stays still. All of life is in constant movement. I had forgotten that. Maybe I forgot because as a human being my life is surrounded by man-made objects, which of course appear to be motionless: books, chairs, things like that. But bodies, even the dead ones, are constantly moving. Maybe the dead ones more than any others. They give up what they were as quickly as possible so that they can go back to being simple minerals. Which is what life is all about. We go through this complicated drama about love and greed and kindness but it's all just so we can die and return to the ground as minerals."

"How can dead bodies move?" Helene asked.

"The maggots and the worms, don't you see?"

"That's a coincidence," Faith said. "Before you got back, William, Harry and I were talking about the sonnets of Keats and I recited this one for him."

Before Faith could begin, Helene went into the kitchen. Poetry, especially when it was written by a great poet, made her nervous.

When I have fears that I may cease to be
   Before my pen has gleaned my teeming brain...

Hearing it a second time, Helene was impressed by the first few lines. Inspired, she said to herself, When I have fears that I will never know... Never know what? When I have fears that I will never know what happens in between the things I see... But that was a relief, wasn't it? How awful it would be to know about everything that happened. What cries I miss, what whispers I don't hear, what words of sorrow are spoken in the rooms I pass... What was she doing with a man who had

chiseled the world away till it was so flat and featureless all he
had to do was count his sexual victories? How could she be
satisfied with a man she couldn't admire?

> And when I feel, fair creature of an hour
>   That I shall never look upon thee more,

William's face was in the shadows, but still, Helene could
sense his agitation.

> ...then on the shore
> Of the wide world I stand alone, and think,

He got up suddenly and went into the bathroom.

"Soup is ready," Helene called. "Bring your glasses and
come on in." She ladled the soup into four deep blue-and-white
bowls, giving each one some potato, celery, and chicken. Then
she crumbled burdock root into each bowl because it had a
dark rich flavor that matched the flavor of the black bread she
had put on the table. Everyone sat down. William came back
and his face was so red it looked like he'd been scrubbing it
with a washcloth. Helene put her napkin in her lap and so did
everyone else. Harry was the first to start eating.

"This sure ain't Campbell's," he said.

"The chicken is so tasty," Faith remarked. "Mine's usually
just like rubber."

William cleared his throat. Helene watched him. She could
see he was making an effort to be sociable. "These chickens
were born in the chicken shed, killed in the backyard, and
cooked in the kitchen. That's the secret."

"I can't get over what that girl did," Helene said to Harry. "When she danced on the roof, was that at night?"

"What girl?" William asked.

"A couple of kids we saw one night over in the Baldwin Building," Helene said.

"Baldwin Mercantile?"

"Right, above Smokes and Jokes."

The stormy expression on William's face had faded away. "I remember when that was a department store. The funny thing is that I just got into the shop a book of poems by the sister of the Baldwin who ran that business into the ground. Eloise."

"Who are these kids?" Faith asked. "Maybe I know them."

"That woman I was telling you about, who's been coming to the bar since before I even owned it..."

"Was the department store still going back then?" William asked.

"Flat out of business. At the time, it made me wonder if I was crazy to think a bar could survive. Course, the hardware store hadn't gone under and there was the restaurant..."

"And," Helene said, "people always like to drink. They might not buy new clothes, but they'll still buy drinks."

"The funny thing is," William broke in, "the mercantile went under because of poor management. The town's economy didn't have anything to do with it. This Bernie Baldwin was a philanderer. Yet his sister wrote poetry. Terrible poetry, of course, but poetry."

"I have a Darryl Baldwin in one of my classes," said Faith. "I wonder if they're related."

"That's the beauty of a small town," William said. "Most people are related and even if they're not, you can be sure they at least know the intimate details of each other's business."

"Not to mention how they're getting into each other's pants," Harry added.

"This girl interests me," Faith said, "the one you say climbed out of the window."

"Me too," Harry said.

"More soup?" asked Helene.

"I don't know. Is there going to be other stuff to eat or is this it?" Harry asked.

"Other stuff?" Helene stood up. She went to the oven and took out two dishes that she brought to the table. One was baked squash and the other was noodles. She also brought over a dish of pickled beets that was made even more colorful by the chopped parsley and carrot she had stirred through it.

"This is absolutely delicious and I'm getting so full." Faith said.

William suddenly looked at her. "Your hair is different. I couldn't tell what was different about you at first, but I knew there was something. You look more formal. I mean, it's very becoming, but I think if I were one of your students I'd take one look at you and know that the time had come to buckle down." Everyone laughed.

"Oh, I don't wear it this way to school. It was just a last-minute idea."

"You usually wear it different?" Harry asked.

Faith blushed. "I actually have curly hair but this gel stuff I put in sometimes makes it look straight."

"Austere, that's the word. You look austere tonight. Do you feel austere?"

Faith put a helping of food on her plate. "Actually, William,

I don't feel austere at all. I feel relaxed. I have a wonderful friend who I am going to see later on tonight so I'm happy. Oh, Helene, this looks and smells utterly delicious."

"I don't think you've told me about him," William said. He was aware of his eyes suddenly, and since he didn't trust himself to look at Faith, he looked down at the table.

"No, I haven't. We always talk about books. Also, I've been a bit reticent about my private life. The reason is my friend is a woman." She didn't dare look at William. She merely sent the information out to the table and kept on eating. What he did, she didn't know. She felt as though she were insulated from all the sounds, captured in a bubble by herself.

Harry started to talk. "I got Stella on the brain," he announced. "I can't stop thinking about her."

The bubble broke. She looked up at them and saw that no one's face had changed. William was eating. She couldn't see his expression. "Stella Doyle?" she asked.

"The girl," Harry said.

"The one who was dancing on the roof?" Helene asked.

"That's the only one I've been talking about," Harry replied testily. "The two ladies I've mentioned this evening are Stella Doyle and her mother, Hattie, who's crazy."

"I know Stella Doyle," Faith said.

"Then I got to tell you something," Harry said. "You know Stella Doyle, you're in the club. The Stella Doyle Club. You gotta be, right? There's no way to know her and shrug her off."

"I don't know her," William said from the end of the table.

Faith tried to catch his eye but he zoomed right past her face when he addressed Harry. I'm a lesbian, she wanted to shout. Do you get that? I'm the only one in this entire town.

"If you're in the Stella Doyle Club you gotta know this. How when she got up on the roof she took her dress off and stark naked, like she was the only one awake in the world, she started dancing. Even from across the street, even at night, she was this picture of beauty, of life, of your dreams making a totally unexpected appearance when you're wide awake."

"Naked?" Helene asked.

"Like I said, purely a nutso thing to do. So I watched and then I went down to the street and talked to her. I figured, hell, wasn't it worth it? Never mind what she might think of me. A dirty old man, a nosy bastard, whatever. I wanted to connect with her, you know what I mean, not in a sexual way. That was the farthest thing from my mind, let me tell you. But you just do the daily grind with your eyes closed most of the time, I mean you try to do the right thing, and all that, and I know I've slipped up occasionally, but this was a time I could have my eyes open and pay attention."

He turned to Faith and William to include them and said, "Usually I never even bother to look out the window. What's to look at on Main Street? But Helene got me started on this thing and like I said, there I was and there she was, like a spirit, an angel, a dream in the pure middle of the night, pulling this gown over her head and tossing it down and then stepping out onto the roof like she's stepping out on a stage. For the moon. It was up there, big and throbbing, a big circle far off in the distance. Me and the girl and the moon. Like I said, I wanted to connect. I wanted to do something for once that didn't have any little extras for me, something completely honest. I wanted to say, hey kid, I know something about doing crazy things and there's something I think you should understand."

He stopped, took a drink. But when he didn't go on again Helene asked, "What should she understand, Harry?"

He seemed surprised that she didn't think he was finished. "Well, just that she should know something about danger. That between this world and the other world there is only the thinnest curtain. One slip and you're through it."

"Yes," Faith said. "One slip. And for Stella Doyle, slipping is an easy thing to do. When I have fears for Stella Doyle." She took a sip of wine and said, "When I have fears of slipping through the curtain, myself or Stella Doyle..."

The table was silent. Suddenly, the room seemed deeper, the colors richer, and everyone sitting there was acutely aware of where they were and what they were thinking.

Helene could feel Uta. Two nights before the second anniversary of her death, her mother was out in the mud room putting her boots on to go outside. Whenever the first snow came, whatever time of day it was, Uta would go outside to greet it. She said snow was a blessing; it was the tears of the angels. That's what she was doing. She'd left the dinner party to be with the snow.

William, who had been seeing Uta so often lately, couldn't resurrect her material body anymore and now that Faith, who had been his only hope, was happily bedded down with a woman, the hole in his life was so deep and dark he wasn't sure he could keep himself from falling inside it.

Faith could feel all parts of herself. The night hummed. It was an extension of her body, a great yielding female space waiting for her.

Harry wasn't planning how to get his cock into Faith's pants (which would be nothing less than a challenge) or under

Helene's dress (always a warm, familiar place) but was out on Main Street. Up in the sky a figure was slumped against a building and with his heart and his soul he was trying to keep her up there.

At last someone moved. It was Helene. She got up and cleared the dishes. Faith stood up to help her. Helene brought coffee to the table and four bowls of pudding, which had been chilling in the refrigerator. She had made a sauce for it, which she took out of the oven where it had been staying warm.

They passed around spoons and cups. Helene poured the coffee. Harry spooned sugar into his. Faith poured cream into hers. There was the smell of the coffee and the tinkling of silverware. Then William pushed his chair back. He slipped down to the floor and walked away.

Helene assumed he would be back in a few minutes so she didn't pay attention. Neither did anyone else. Pudding wobbled on spoons. Harry sighed. Faith murmured. Helene said, "When I was a little girl in Dresden we had an enormous black enamel stove in our kitchen and my mother would simmer pudding in a big white pot and sauce for it in another pot and I would come home from playing outside in the afternoons and find the kitchen table set with the beautiful painted bowls that had been in my mother's family and which she had inherited from my grandmother and in the bowls there would be this same red strawberry sauce except they were German strawberries we would have picked in the garden my grandmother kept and which I had helped my mother to can, and under the sauce there was this same butterscotch pudding. When I was a little girl that's what I looked forward to when I came home from playing outside. We would hear the bells ringing in the cathedral down the street and the sounds of Frau Singer's piano would come up to us from downstairs. That is my memory of Dresden. Frau Singer and her family disappeared one afternoon because they were Jews. When we came home after shopping one day they were gone and all of their furniture and books and clothes were being loaded into a truck by a soldier," She stopped talking. Frau Singer and her tall happy husband. Their two little boys who used to play with her in the garden behind the apartment house. She could see the whole family walking along the street together. "Pudding is the only thing left. I also have a book of my mother's, a book of memories from before the bombing."

Faith said, "That's a terrible loss. What the Allies did to you people in Dresden. I understand they've rebuilt the city but I'm sure it's not the same."

"No, it's not the same," Helene said. "It couldn't be."

"The only pudding I ever had was out of the box. Royal. You ever had that, Helene? Wouldn't even call it pudding. Facsimile. But not pudding. No siree. This is the first time I've ever had the real thing. And I got to tell you something. I hope you ladies won't mind. What this pudding makes me think of, the way it wobbles but stays firm, the way it's smooth but solid. That's the thing about it, smooth but solid, wobbly but firm..."

"Yes!" Faith said, lifting up a spoonful. "And the cold pudding with the hot sauce! It's a bowl full of contradictions!"

"What it is is a woman's bosom. Everything that a woman's bosom is."

"Smooth but solid, wobbly but firm. You're right about that," Faith said.

Helene spoke up next. "Isn't it funny the way one day everything is in place and it's lovely and comfortable and gives you so much pleasure. Like the city you live in, or a person you love. And the next day it's not there at all. And there wasn't a warning of any sort. I was just thinking what a funny thing that is."

Harry and Faith agreed. Then another silence fell on the table. Helene said, "You will have to forgive me for these unhappy thoughts. Monday is the anniversary of my mother's death."

"October eleventh?" Faith asked.

"She was in a car crash two years ago and I'm filled with memories right now. What happened to William?" She stood up suddenly and said, "Have more pudding. I think I need to find him."

Helene walked through the living room and down the dark hallway. The bathroom door was standing open, which meant the only other place William could have gone was his bedroom. The door was closed and there wasn't any light coming out from under it. She knocked softly.

"Come in," he said, so she opened it. The glow from the outside light spilled in through his window. He was sitting in the chair at his desk so she sat down on the bed across from him. "Is it *Mutter*?"

"It's unbearable."

"Yes," Helene said. "But I made a wonderful dessert and our friends are wondering where you disappeared to."

"I can't go out there."

"They'll be going soon. Come out for ten minutes and then tell them you're tired and excuse yourself. They'll understand."

"She didn't want anyone to know what we meant to one another. She was ashamed of me. That's why we never married."

"She loved you very much," Helene said. "You were good friends."

"We were lovers." He looked at Helene but she was quiet. Then she said, "I guess I never knew that."

"She never told you?"

"She wouldn't tell such a thing to her daughter. It wouldn't have been proper."

"She was ashamed of it."

"No, my mother was a very private person. She didn't announce things. She was very simple. She just took what she had, day by day. Isn't that what she did?"

"I don't know. We didn't talk philosophy. She never felt comfortable with English. After all those years she never really learned it. If I had known German maybe she would have married me. If I had been taller maybe she would have married me."

"Don't you see?" Helene reached across the dark space to find William's hand but he wouldn't give it to her. "Don't you see? It had nothing to do with that. She was afraid to proclaim anything. Because once you say what you have, once you say where you are, you lose it. She couldn't have gone through that again. She kept it a secret because she thought that was the only way it would stay with her. It was the only way she thought she would stay safe. She'd lost everything once, she'd lost our two fathers, her city, her family, her friends, and she was afraid it would happen again. Don't you see that, Papa?"

He put his head into his hands and the cries that came out of him were loud and anguished. It was a weeping that was rusty, clogged, horrible to listen to. It didn't even sound human. But Helene wasn't frightened. She simply sat on the end of the bed. She knew she belonged there with him, that he was her true substitute father and he needed her to witness what he was feeling.

"I can't go out there," he said finally.

"No, you can't. You stay here. I will tell them and they'll go home." She kissed his forehead. "My mother loved you. She couldn't marry you because she was afraid it would make you disappear. Everything she had loved had disappeared. She didn't want the same thing to happen to you, so she was very careful to keep you a secret. You must believe that."

In the kitchen they were talking softly, drinking coffee. "Is William all right?" Faith asked.

"It was a combination of two things," Helene said. "My mother and not feeling well. He went to bed. He asked me to tell you good night for him."

Faith stood up. "It's been such a lovely evening. Wonderful food and wonderful company and I'm so sorry William isn't feeling well. But I understand, of course. I hope he gets some rest. Do you think it's still snowing? Helene, you put my coat somewhere."

"Right here," Helene said, going to the closet. She helped Faith into it and walked her outside.

The snow was still coming down but the flakes were smaller because it had turned colder. They glistened in Helene's hair when she came back into the kitchen.

Harry brushed the snow off her. "Sure, the pudding was

good," he said. "Better than pudding in the box. But it wasn't as good as you are. Come into town with me. Come spend the night. It's the weekend."

She didn't even hesitate. "Will you help me with the dishes? I'll come, but I want to leave the kitchen clean for William."

Thirty-Six

W hat she saw the first morning she woke up in Paris was
a valley with its creases filled by fog. Peering out the
window at the first daylight while Gunter and Helene still
slept, she caught her breath at the beauty of it. She had imagined that America would be a place of shops and busy streets,
like an enormous New York City, and had been surprised to
see so many miles of empty land when they came out on the
bus. And here was more of it. It reminded her of the valley
where her grandmother's family house was situated, the place
she had gone all the summers of her childhood and where her
grandmother had taught her the plants. As she looked, the sun
was already drying out the fog and she could see the contours
of the land. Such longing she felt! Such meadows and hillsides!

Uta put on the same clothes she had worn the day before,
first a thin cotton summer dress, then a heavy corduroy skirt
and a long-sleeved shirt over it with a heavy sweater on top.

Dressing in layers was a habit she had adopted for the trip to lighten her suitcase. She knew she'd be carrying the suitcase again that day, as soon as Dagmar arrived to pick them up. With shoes in hand, she tiptoed downstairs. It was only the second American house she had ever been in, the first being the abandoned house the man had taken her to. She wondered what Dagmar's house would be like. Or where it was. She would telephone him all day long so she could be reunited as quickly as possible with the only person in this enormous country who knew who she was. Although it was very nice in this man's house, she didn't want to inconvenience him any longer.

Sitting down at the kitchen table, she pulled on the same stockings and two pairs of socks. She walked to the bottom of the stairway to make sure the children were still asleep. All quiet.

The back door opened easily. But she had forgotten it wasn't outdoors right away. It was the room filled with stacks of wood. She couldn't remember where the door to it was and it was hard to see in the darkness because there wasn't a window. All of a sudden, she felt frightened. Where had the door to the kitchen gone? She groped for the handle. Right there, it was right there. "You are all right," she whispered to herself. She opened the kitchen door and let in some of the light from the house and right away—such a silly woman—she could see inside the wood room and find the door to the outside.

It was chilly. The grass was wet with dew. She stood at the door and looked across the valley. Mist still hung in the distance, but up close everything was clear. The sun even had a touch of warmth to it. A field sloped down to the road and on the other side of the road it was flat. She walked into the grass and then into the field, which was all goldenrod. The stalks were brown and dried with the little seeds on the gray flower heads just waiting for anything to brush against them and carry them off. After just a few steps, her sweater was covered. No matter, it was her first American goldenrod, her first American field, and though it wasn't a place she was going to be in for longer than a couple of days—because Dagmar would be found—she felt sudden peace. Here at last. Safe on the other side. She wanted to do something to commemorate. So she lay down in the field, getting the seeds in her hair and on her stockings, and looked up into the bright blue of the sky. The damp ground hardly penetrated her layers. She closed her eyes and felt the dawn on her eyelids. *Danke, meine Erde.* Thank you, my earth.

Thirty-Seven

"Jesus Fucking Christ," Hattie said when she got off work and saw the white parking lot. "October eighth. Couldn't it have waited another month?" She didn't have a brush or a scraper, but it was so soft she could wipe it off the windshield with her sleeve. She didn't do the back because it was too much trouble and she only wiped off the front window on the driver's side. She didn't wipe off the passenger windows, but when she opened the door, the snow slid off onto her bare hands. Gloves were an item she no longer bothered with. She scooched under the steering wheel, her coat catching between her legs in the annoying way it always did, and closed the door. Inside the dark car, she set her pocketbook beside her and unsnapped the top. In the bottom, under her wallet in a plastic makeup bag, was a Three Musketeers bar. She took a bite before turning the key and as the engine warmed up, she ate the whole thing to fortify herself for the drive home. Someday she would just stay in the parking lot. When Stella was grown up, there wouldn't be a reason for going home. She would just lock the doors and sit in the parking lot until it was morning.

At the street, she leaned over the passenger side and rolled down the window to take off the snow, and finding the coast clear, made a left turn. The way home was easy. She stayed on one road for five miles, and then made two turns.

Nobody else was out. There weren't even any tire tracks. She felt as though she were sailing forth on a white ocean, the big car moving smoothly and soundlessly, the roar of its muffler imperceptible in the dark cavern inside where the green numbers on the speedometer were the only illumination.

She took the first turn too fast, and the back swung out, but she got on course again and sailed the ship straight into the second turn, which was their driveway. As she walked up to the porch she noticed that the lights at the back of the house were on and a truck was pulled up to the back door. This sight was so inexplicable it occurred to her that she was imagining it. But she didn't think so.

Once she got into the house she could tell it wasn't a mind trick. The kitchen was lit up like broad daylight and two boys were walking the refrigerator side to side onto a hand truck that Stella was maneuvering. They seemed to know what they were doing. In fact, she wondered if the ability to move heavy furniture was carried in the genes because that's what Rafael had done after he left them. He worked for a moving company. She had once seen him carry a queen-size bed through a tiny house and out the front door as easily as though it were a little love seat. Stella seemed to have the same confidence.

With snow so early in the season, Hattie felt depressed, so

she simply went upstairs into her bedroom. After a while she must have fallen asleep because when she woke up, sometime later, she heard an engine come to life right below her window. She wondered if her car was blocking the truck, but decided the driveway was on the other side of the house so there wasn't any reason to be concerned about it.

When she woke up next, Stella was coming into the room. "I need your car keys," she said.

"My jacket," Hattie replied. She didn't have to ask what for. She knew. Rafael had parked a moving truck on the lawn and now that the house was empty, he needed to drive it far away. The only thing stopping him was her giant pink car. Stella could move it although Stella couldn't drive. No matter, Hattie thought to herself. The girl was smart. She'd watched her mother so many times she'd know how to do it automatically.

Thirty-Eight

~~

The next morning the sun was out and the snow had melted. They drove the appliances to the pawn shop in Darryl's uncle's truck. The man at the pawn shop gave them a hundred and fifty dollars for the refrigerator and fifty for the stove. Stella's wallet bulged. Driving back home in the empty truck, she asked Darryl to pull over.

He turned from the road to look at her.

"Just pull over, I've got to talk to you."

"Sure, after this car passes."

He pulled the truck onto the shoulder and turned off the motor.

She put her hands in her pockets and looked at the speed limit sign in front of them. "What if she refuses to go? She's so stubborn. She doesn't like to change and I'm just scared that this whole thing is going to collapse and I'll never get her to go."

He touched her sleeve, coaxed her hand into his. "Listen,

Stella, just talk to her. Sit her down in the kitchen and tell her why you want her to do it. I'll tell you the thing I'm worried about—her driving."

"She's fine if she's sober. That's why we have to leave today."

He pulled his wallet out of his pocket and said, "I don't have much. But take this fifty dollars, okay? It'll buy you a couple more bags of food. And be careful and stay calm and don't fall in love with any guys over in Chicago because I'll be sitting here waiting for you to get back, okay?"

"I don't know. I don't know about this whole thing. I mean, am I crazy for thinking we can do this? I'm not crazy, am I? We can camp in the car right in the hospital parking lot. It's probably huge and they'll never see us. And I'll find enough to do. I'm taking all my schoolbooks. And she'll get better. And if this doesn't do it, I'm going to have to give up. I'm going to have to leave. And I don't know what's going to happen to her." She leaned over and looked into his face.

The Cadillac was still in the driveway. As she walked down the path, giddy from their quick fuck in the front seat of the truck while they were sitting along the highway, she locked away the sensations in her body and focused on the house instead. It looked deserted, but only because the sun had turned the windows black. She opened the front door and walked through the living room to the cloud of cigarette smoke that wafted out of the kitchen.

"Where'd he take them?" Hattie called out.

The kitchen looked enormous without the appliances. The linoleum was brighter in the empty dusty spaces. Yet her mother sat at the table in front of a cup of coffee and an ashtray as always. She was still in her bathrobe.

"We sold them in Sharon."

"What for?"

"Two hundred dollars."

"That jerk, he robbed me once already. Why'd you let him in here?"

"It was me and Darryl. Darryl helped put the stuff onto the truck. I couldn't have done it without him."

"That man doesn't need help," her mother said bitterly. "I've seen him move a queen-size bed through a house smaller than this one like it was a goddamned love seat."

"Darryl was doing it, Mom. I asked him to. You and me need the money."

"For what?"

"We're going to get you well."

Hattie shook a cigarette out of the pack on the table and put it between her lips. Then she took it out again and with the cigarette hanging off her hand like a crooked finger said, "I haven't had anything to eat but crackers and soda for two days."

"No, Mom. Listen, I'm taking you to Chicago to a clinic. We're going to be there for two weeks, the two of us; I'm going to stay with you."

"And how much is this place going to cost us?"

"It's just a twenty-five dollar registration fee. The rest is free because it's connected to a hospital and it's government funded."

"That's what they tell you. But then once you get there they hand you a bill for a thousand dollars. I know what those clinics are like. They don't work, I've tried them."

"I know. But this one is different. This one does acupuncture."

Hattie narrowed her eyes and her face looked even larger. "Acu what?"

"Puncture."

"That's not that thing with the needles?"

Stella nodded. Then she reached out for her mother's hand and said, "Please."

"If there's one thing this body ain't going to do it's get stuck with needles. I promised myself that a long time ago. Needles are out. I've been punched and kicked and slapped around, but I'll tell you one thing. I might be big and puffy but I ain't going to be treated like a pincushion."

"I think acupuncture needles are different from regular needles. They're really small and narrow. They're like hairs."

"Sorry, kiddo. Your mom's doing okay, anyway. I'm off the sugar and the carbos. I don't need that stuff."

"You're not going to have a refrigerator or stove unless you come to Chicago."

"I don't need a refrigerator or stove. We hardly used them anyway."

"Mom..."

"That man fucked me over once and I just laid down and let him fuck me over again. Never trust someone who's not your own race. And some hell of a father he's been to you, that bastard."

"It wasn't him, Mom. He hasn't been here. It was Darryl. My father had nothing to do with it."

"Like hell he didn't."

"It was my idea and Darryl put them on a truck and I sold them for money for Chicago."

"That's where the clinic is," Hattie said in a neutral tone.

"Yes, and you're going there for two weeks."

"Those places are for people who can't control themselves. I have a system."

Stella remembered how she felt when she discovered her mother had been on Main Street in her bathrobe. She saw herself standing in front of the class feeling like she was going to cry in front of everyone and her face grew hot with shame. "Do you know what it's like? Do you? Do you have any idea? Do you even care? Well, I'll tell you something. I've never had a mother and I'm sick of it and I am going to get myself a mother and that's why I sold the appliances and I'm not going to get them back unless you go to Chicago."

"And I'll tell you something," Hattie said, pushing her chair back and standing up. "I raised you by myself and I worked and I kept a roof over your head and I took care of you when you were sick and..."

"And I want that mother back! She hasn't been around here for years. And I'll tell *you* something. You're losing your daughter. I'm not going to live here if you go on like this. I'm moving out. I have another place to live and I don't need you. You can just stay here and diet all by yourself. Because I'm going to leave and you can just keep on with your bags of potato chips and your soda and keep your own self company. And I hope you go crazy and they lock you up."

"Don't you talk to me!"

"It's the truth."

Holding her bathrobe closed, Hattie said, "You can get out of here, little girl."

"Oh sure. Go ahead. Send me away as soon as things get uncomfortable."

"You are not going to talk to me like that in my own house."
Stella blocked her. "This is it, Mom. Something is going to
happen today. Either we pack our bags and go to Chicago or
I pack my stuff and move out."

Hattie let go of her bathrobe and fumbled in her pocket for
a lighter. She held it up to her cigarette and squinted her eyes
against the smoke. "Where would you go?" she asked softly.

"I'm going to live at a teacher's house. There's a room
waiting for me over there and I'm going to go because I can't
stand it anymore."

"So who do you think I show up at work for every day?
Who do you think I drag myself through this lousy existence
for, if it isn't you? I would have killed myself a long time ago."

"That's funny, because you're hardly living now. You know
something?"

"Tell me," Hattie said sarcastically, the cigarette burning
between her fingers.

"You look like shit. You don't even know what it's like to
be a part of the world anymore. You're just all resentment."

Hattie took the cigarette out of her mouth. Her face
slumped like she was going to cry. Her eyes got bigger. The red
veins around them became more pronounced. "Stel...look, it
hasn't been easy. I just wish for once it would be easy. I'm sick
to death of climbing the goddamn mountain every day. I'm
tired of worrying about things. I want a rest."

"I'll take you to Chicago and you can have a rest. Come on,
you can get your body back, you can be a real mother." Stella
tried to put her arms around Hattie.

"You don't want something like me touching you."

"I do, Mom, I do." When Hattie didn't move, she picked up

her mother's arm and draped it around her neck. It was warm and heavy and had a slightly rancid smell to it. With the arm over her shoulder, Stella walked into the big body and said, "We can do this together."

"Nothing's that bad, Stel. Don't ask me to change. Everything hurts so goddamn much I can't do it. I'm just fine the way I am. I have a system. I'm losing weight, Stel, every day. I'm almost there."

"Mom, don't do this to yourself. Don't do it to me. Come upstairs and we'll pack your things and then we'll pack mine and we'll go to this clinic, okay? I'll take you away and everything'll be all right and you'll get your rest."

"That fucking man. To come over here and steal stuff right out of our kitchen. It was some slimy Mexican deal. They get stuff out of the U.S. and melt it down to rebuild, hell, I don't know, buses, apartment houses, they'll build anything out of anything because they're like vultures, those people."

Stella steered her mother toward the steps. "He really had the nerve, didn't he? How'd he think we could manage?"

"He didn't think," Hattie hissed. "He never thought about anything."

"We're going to be different from that, aren't we? We're going to think things through and plan ahead."

Hattie climbed the steps ahead of her. She went slowly, breathing hard, stopping along the way to rest. When they were at the top, Stella said, "You pick out enough really warm clothes for two weeks. Really warm, Mom, because we're going to be sleeping in the car, okay? I'm going to pack clothes for myself and find us blankets. We're going to try to leave here in half an hour."

Hattie went into her room but she came out a moment later. "Stel, I just thought of something. I have no idea where the key is."

"What key?"

"The key to the front door. We've got to lock this place up."

"Mom, there isn't anything here that anyone would want to steal."

"If that man took the appliances, he's going to come back for the furnace. I know him. He doesn't give up till he strips you clean."

"I don't think so. I think he's long gone. You know what he told me, Mom?"

"What did that lying bastard say to you? And don't believe it for a second."

"He said he was driving our appliances down to Argentina, that's where he was taking them."

"That's a good place. If he's in Argentina it's going to be a long time before he ever pokes his dirty lying face in here again." She went into her room where Stella heard her say, "Argentina, I wonder what kind of scam he's got going down there." She shuffled out to Stella's door. "Do you think it's drugs? Is he packing drugs in our refrigerator?"

"No, Mom. He said he needed refrigerators to build houses for...well, have you heard about these Vietnamese pigs? They're like dogs they're so intelligent."

"Pigs? Why do pigs have to stay cold?"

"They don't plug the refrigerators in, they just use them as little huts, like. And it'll take him months to get them down there because they go by boat. So we can leave the door open, he won't be back. Go get ready, Mom, he won't bother us."

Stella pictured a meadow filled with refrigerators. Little brown pigs poked their faces out of the doorways, grunting softly. Would it be winter in Argentina when it was autumn in Chicago?

She folded up some jeans and sweaters and dug out her long underwear. She took the pillow from her bed and rolled up the blanket. Her clothes she stuffed in a pillowcase along with her toiletry things and a couple of towels. She carried everything down to the couch. She grabbed her knapsack with all her books and threw that on the pile. Then she went back up to her mother's room. Hattie was lying on the bed. The shades were pulled. She hadn't packed anything.

Stella sat down next to her. Maybe she should just move out. Maybe Hattie was too far gone. "You old piece of shit." She went to the window and pulled down on the shade to make it go up. But it didn't. The spring was shot. So in the thick yellow shadows she opened her mother's closet. There wasn't anything on the hangers. Instead, there was a heap of clothes on top of the dresser. Of everything, it was that that made her the saddest. There was nothing to do but sort through it, and in the false evening of the room, with the smell of her mother's body suffocating her, look for a pair of pants. She tried some drawers but she should have known that they would all be empty. So she threw things onto the floor until she had uncovered enough warm clothes. She stuffed them into a pillowcase and went to the bathroom to gather her mother's things. She packed a lipstick and eye shadow because maybe her mother would start to care about how she looked. There were some quilts in the hallway closet that she slung over her shoulder, and, picking up the pillowcase, she carried a second load down to the couch.

Packing the car was the next step. She went out with a paper bag first to pick up the junk on the floor. There were old grocery bags full of empty cookie boxes. There were soda and candy wrappers and a bunch of clothes on the back seat. She found an open bag of fudge cookies under a blanket. There were pieces of cookie on the floor. She swept it all into the bag of trash, which she emptied into the barrel by the kitchen door. Then she took out a broom to get up the crumbs. Finally, it was as clean as she could make it. It took three trips to carry everything from the couch out to the car and by then it was four o'clock. She went upstairs to wake Hattie. She hadn't moved. Her eyes were closed and her hands were still clasped under her head. "Mom!"

Stella sat down next to her and shook her shoulders. "We're going to Chicago and we have to leave. Get up!"

"I want to call the police," Hattie said, opening her eyes.

"Mom, wake up, we're going to Chicago. We're going to get you well, come on."

"Chicago. You know, I haven't been there in years, Stella. They have a wonderful aquarium we can go to." She sat up and put her hand on Stella's arm. "A man can't walk into your house and take your appliances. Even if he's down in Argentina, the police have to be notified. Because you know and I know that it's probably drugs."

"No, Mom, come on, let's go."

"I have to get dressed. You pack the car and I'll get dressed."

"It is packed. You've been asleep. We just have to get into the car."

"Let me get pants on."

"Quick, Mom." Stella ran downstairs and brought up the

pile of clothes she'd brought in from the car. "Here, Mom, there's pants in here."

Leaning on the bedpost, Hattie pulled them up her body slowly. When she took off her bathrobe, her enormous breasts lay collapsed on her belly. Stella threw her a bra and a shirt. Then she handed Hattie a ratty white sweater that had been in the car.

"I can't wear this," Hattie said. "Chicago is a very sophisticated city."

"I packed you two others. You're okay. You can wear this one while you're driving."

"Have you seen my shoes?"

"They're probably in the kitchen. I'll go get them."

But they weren't in the kitchen. Or the living room. She ran back up and looked in the bathroom. "I don't see them, Mom."

"I can't go to Chicago without shoes."

"Well, where did you take them off?"

"I wore boots yesterday because it was snowing."

"So maybe you left your shoes at work."

"We'll have to go get them."

"No, Mom. Put on your socks. And you can wear your slippers or your boots, but we're not going to the supermarket." Stella expected her to argue, but Hattie put on her slippers like an obedient child.

When they got out to the car, Hattie's face was red with the effort of walking. "I can't find my keys."

Stella ran back in the house and found them on the kitchen counter where Hattie had set them down the night before.

"We need gas," Hattie said as she wrapped her coat around her and squeezed in under the steering wheel.

"Just a minute, Mom. Just sit right there. I'll be right back." Stella opened the door on her side and went around to the back of the car where she knelt down and picked up a handful of cold mud. She smeared it over the license plate. Then she got back inside and said, "We're going to stop at the gas station on the outside of town."

Hattie pumped the accelerator and the engine roared through the rusted muffler. "How far is it to Chicago?"

"I don't know. Don't you?"

"Must be about ten hours."

When they got to the gas station, Hattie turned and looked at her daughter because whenever they were out together, Stella was the one who did the gas. Stella put the nozzle in the hole and let it go until the tank was full. The meter said twenty-two dollars. She felt the wad of bills in her pants pocket and decided that twenty-two dollars could buy them a night at a motel for a shower. She hopped back into the car and Hattie, assuming she had paid, pulled out. Stella checked to see if anyone was coming out of the station after them, but the door stayed shut. Of course, they might have been standing at the desk, dialing the police. "We want 90 west. Do you know how to get there?"

"90 west," Hattie repeated. "I think one of these roads up here goes into it."

"There aren't any signs."

"This is the old way, the back way. We're not close enough for signs. But it'll run into 90 west and if it doesn't, we'll just take this all the way into Ohio. I'm so glad we're getting out of here, Stella. New scenery is always refreshing. Want some music?" Hattie turned the dial for the radio but nothing happened.

"There's something wrong with the electrical. It's those god-damned mice."

"Mice?"

"They're chewing the wires. I saw one scurrying around yesterday when I opened the door. I must have left food inside."

"What wire did they chew?"

"Must have chewed the wire to the radio."

The road stretched ahead of them, a black slice going into the hills. Hattie put her foot down on the accelerator and the big car rocketed forward. The speedometer climbed to seventy and Hattie started to laugh. "What's that fool doing on a ship with our refrigerator and stove? It's all land, isn't it? We could go after him."

Stella smiled. "There's the Panama Canal. That's a minor interruption."

"Hell, this old car looks more like a boat anyway."

Stella looked out the window. The hills were turning blue as ribbons of darkness floated down out of the clouds. There were trees on the ridges, dark skeletons. Two hawks dipped low and circled upwards again, making intersecting loops. The road plunged into speckled dusk as it passed through a line of beech trees. On the other side, the sky hung low and heavy. As they streaked underneath it, the car plunged into a dip in the road and the frame started to bounce up and down. "What's it doing?" Stella asked. "What's going on?"

"Oh, it's the struts or suspension or something like that that starts with an s. Shocks, that's what they are. The shocks are gone. It happens when you hit something irregular in the road."

"Is that okay?"

"Long as we don't lurch down into a pothole." Hattie

stared out of the window with confidence, her hands at the top of the wheel. "Pigs! That man knows no limits."

"Shouldn't you turn the lights on? It's getting dark."

Hattie pulled out the lever on the dashboard.

"Did they go on?"

"They did, you just can't see them. It's not dark enough yet."

"You're sure this road goes to Ohio? Because I don't see any signs for 90."

"As long as it's headed west, we're okay. In fact, sometimes these back roads are more direct."

They passed a barn that was in the process of sliding into the earth, its timbers splayed under the weight of the collapsed roof. "So, Mom, tell me what my father used to look like. Because the other day, you know, when he came to steal our stuff, I didn't think he was so handsome."

Hattie laughed. "Oh God, he was! He was the handsomest man I ever laid my eyes on. Dark, just like you. He had thick dark hair. Big hands, narrow hips, a wide chest. A beauty, Stella, and back then, I wasn't so bad-looking myself. We were a handsome couple. Things should have worked out. They should have worked out."

"What color eyes did he have?"

"Green, like yours. Green and mysterious. I fell in love with that man the first time I saw him. I lost all my sense in that first second. If anyone had warned me that he was going to ruin my life I wouldn't have listened. He put a spell on me. Those Latins, if there's anything they know, it's how to romance. From that night on, I was putty in his hands. Christ, I would have followed him anywhere."

"So who named me?"

"You named yourself. You looked like Stella. I just saw you and thought, Stella by Starlight, and there you were, smiling up at me."

"Did he like the name?"

"I don't know. I suppose he did, it sounds sort of Spanish. But he never said one way or the other. He was a man who didn't talk much."

"Mom, it's almost six o'clock and I don't think your lights are on."

Hattie checked the lever again. It was pulled out. Then she stepped on the button for the high beams. Nothing happened. "What's wrong with this thing? Goddamned mice. They must have chewed through that wire, too. Well, there's hardly any traffic on this road and we probably have another hour of dusk. These old cars, they use gas, but they never wear out. It's just little things, like the electrical. But that was the mice, Stella. So, what's he going to say when we walk side by side into Argentina? Now that's a face I can't wait to get a look at."

"Mom, it's almost dark and we've got to have lights."

"Argentina's a long way off, honey. Let's at least get to Ohio before we pull over. Don't forget, this car is a light color. We're glowing like a lamp, Stella, a lighthouse in a sea of darkness, believe me."

"We're going to Chicago, Mom. For two weeks, then we can go to Argentina."

"That's right, hon, Chicago. To get us a Vietnamese pig. Then we'll go down and find one of them refrigerators to keep it in and lie on the beach a little and get us a tan and you can swim and do that thing they do with the boards in the ocean. It'll be hot and beautiful."

Strips of darkness lay over the landscape and the long nose of the car, bouncing with their speed, took them westwards. Stella watched the needle on the speedometer jiggle up and down between 80 and 85. She relaxed her grip on the door handle. This was how it always was. Her life slipped into the groove that pulled things along too recklessly. She wasn't even scared. It was only another one of Darryl's paintings. A pink car sailing through the empty land, the inside of the car filled with flowers—huge red geraniums, black tulips, sprigs of purple lilacs. They were bursting out of the windows.

When it was so dark Hattie could no longer see, she nosed the car into a field. Stella didn't know if it was New York State or Pennsylvania or Ohio. She let her mother have the back seat and discovered how to get comfortable in the front. But she didn't fall asleep right away. While Hattie's congested breathing took over the tiny space, Stella sat against the door remembering the way Harry had stood on the street and held her up, the way Faith had made her eat a bowl of soup at the restaurant, the way Darryl had given her an extra fifty dollars. She felt like they were with her on this crazy trip.

Thirty-Nine

On the anniversary of the day Uta died, Helene woke up early. She came down to the kitchen. An icy rain was spilling out of the clouds and the kitchen was so dark she set a fat red candle in the candleholder and put it on the table. She took the notebook off the shelf and let chance guide her to a page. She read the first entry:

In the summer children swam in the river below the Terrasse. I would have taken Helene there when she was older so that she could wade into the cold green water and then lie on her blanket on the grassy shore and dry off in the sun. On Saturdays, quartets played all day long and we would listen to music and birds and the laughter of children.

Swimming and listening to music. If things had happened differently, that's what she might have done. She returned the book, gathered her coat and her purse, and left for the post office.

• • •

When William woke up, long after Helene had left, the candle was still burning. He cut two slices of rye bread and put them in the toaster. He put dog food in Buster's bowl and for a treat poured a little bit of Helene's chicken soup over it. He spread jam on his bread and sat down at the table and watched the flame. He thought he might be able to feel her, but he couldn't, she was truly gone. He sat at the table in his small and limited body and looked at the light. After awhile, he got up and walked into the living room. He opened the door to Uta's bedroom but all of her things were gone and the room smelled like paint because Helene had started to fix it up. He crossed to the window. The snow had brought down the last of the red leaves on the ash trees and the hillside was stark and bare. He walked out of the room and into the kitchen and looked out of the window there. The yellow leaves on the maple behind the house were all down. They lay on the grass, a brilliant yellow patch that would slowly turn brown with the weather. He went back to the table and as he finished breakfast he remembered how on the nights she stayed in his bed with him, he would put his arms around her and get as close to her as possible. When he thought he was as close as possible he would still find pockets of space between them and so he would slide in even closer to fill them up. She would turn herself towards him and fit her chest against his chest, her legs against his legs, and they would fall asleep like that, their bodies locked together.

A tall man would never have doubted it. But it was not a tall man, it was he, the one who didn't trust anything, who never forgot that he didn't look like other people, who thought the world and the woman were treating him differently. It was he, William, the one who had wasted such precious time.

8/99